"Hey, Crys! Wait up!"

Crystal stopped in the middle of the street. There was no way in the world she wouldn't wait for Evan. So what if the light had just changed and traffic was whizzing around her?

"Hi," she said brightly.

Evan raked back his hair and gave her the biggest smile she had seen since Alison dumped him. "Okay if I walk the rest of the way to school with you?"

"Sure," Crystal said. Her heart was doing little flip-flops as the light changed again and they walked along together.

"Alison called last night!" Evan burst out. He spun around, walking backwards and grinning down at her.

Crystal's spirits took a sudden nosedive.

"She...she did?" Crystal asked in a faltering voice. "What did she want?"

"Just to talk," said Evan. He was still grinning like crazy. "Isn't that terrific?"

Listen in on all the *BOY TALK*!

And coming in July 1995:

Boy Talk™

#2
DUDE IN DISTRESS

by Betsy Haynes

BULLSEYE BOOKS
Random House ⌂ New York

For Betty Berkowitz, friends forever

A BULLSEYE BOOK PUBLISHED BY RANDOM HOUSE, INC.

Copyright © 1995 by Betsy Haynes. Cover art copyright © 1995 by Aleta Jenks. All rights reserved under International and Pan-American Copyright Conventions. Published in the United States by Random House, Inc., New York, and simultaneously in Canada by Random House of Canada Limited, Toronto.

Library of Congress Catalog Card Number: 94-67696
ISBN: 0-679-86023-1
RL: 5.0

Manufactured in the United States of America   10 9 8 7 6 5 4 3 2 1

BOY TALK™ is a trademark of Random House, Inc., and Betsy Haynes

Crystal Britton set her schoolbooks on the desk in her bedroom and glanced down at the cover of her notebook. CB + EB, she had written.

Sighing, she turned to her two best friends, Joni Sparkman and Su-Su McCarthy. "Do you realize that if I marry Evan Byrnes my initials won't change?" she said. "They'll still be CB."

Su-Su flipped her long red hair over her shoulder. "Have you told Alison Hamel that? She goes steady with Evan, remember?"

"I know he goes out with her," Crystal said, frowning. "But he does live next door, and we've been good friends our whole lives. When we were really little—like three or four—he used to chase me around the yard and kiss me. He actually made me cry!" Crystal groaned. "I sure was a dumb little kid.

But maybe someday he'll want to kiss me again, and I'll still get a shot at becoming Crystal Byrnes."

"And if I marry Beau, I'll be Joni Maguire," said Joni. "I think Maguire is such a romantic name."

"Well, I'd kill for a boyfriend!" said Su-Su. "But I'm not sure I want to get married, especially if it means changing my name. Then I'd be somebody else. I mean, Susan Suzanna McCarthy is who I am." Shooting a quick grin at Joni, she added, "I think *you* should marry Kevin Maloney. Then you'd be Joni Maloney!"

Joni grabbed a pillow from Crystal's bed and threw it at Su-Su, missing her by a foot. "Puh*leez!* Kevin Maloney is *scum!*"

"Hey, guys, it's almost three-thirty. Time for Boy Talk!" said Crystal, pointing to her watch.

It was Friday afternoon, and the three seventh graders had gone straight to Crystal's house after school. Every day from three-thirty to four-thirty, they ran a secret telephone hot line called Boy Talk. No one at Sunshine Beach Middle School in Sunshine Beach, Florida, knew who was behind Boy Talk, which made it even more fun. Kids could ask for advice for their own romance problems and at the same time listen in on their classmates' problems.

Boy Talk had been Joni's idea. Joni had short dark hair and a mind like a detective. She also had a boyfriend named Beau Maguire, and a few weeks ago she had thought she was losing him. The three girls had seen an ad in a teen magazine for a national hot line called Romance Rap and dialed it up so that Joni could get some advice about Beau. But instead they'd listened to other girls' problems—and run up a whopping phone bill of $72.95! After that, Joni went into action and thought up Boy Talk, which was totally *free*.

Sometimes Crystal had to pinch herself to believe how successful the hot line was so far. All they had done to start it up was leave flyers around school announcing it.

♡ ♡ ♡ ♡ ♡ ♡ ♡ ♡ ♡ ♡ ♡ ♡ ♡ ♡ ♡

BOY TALK

♡ *Totally confidential! Absolutely free!*
♡ *Romance! Dating! Friendship!*
♡ *Share your secrets with other teens!*
♡ *Ask for help with your boyfriend problems!*
♡ *Give advice and be a best friend to someone else!*

CALL 555-3902

After school Monday–Friday, 3:30–4:30

♡ ♡ ♡ ♡ ♡ ♡ ♡ ♡ ♡ ♡ ♡ ♡ ♡ ♡ ♡

Even though it made Crystal nervous, the girls used the answering machine in Mr. Britton's office. Crystal, who was only four feet eleven, with honey-colored hair and a dimple in her left cheek, was also incredibly caring and soft-hearted. That explained why Joni and Su-Su had been able to talk her into using her father's private answering machine.

Mornings Mr. Britton used the office, which had once been a bedroom, to write his newspaper column, but afternoons he taught political science at the local college. His answering machine was hooked to an unlisted phone number that was separate from the Brittons' home number.

Every afternoon the girls removed Mr. Britton's greeting and tape from the answering machine and replaced it with their own. Then, for one whole hour, they sat back while kids called in to record their problems or to record advice.

Su-Su had taped the Boy Talk greeting in an incredibly bogus English accent that made Crystal laugh every time she heard it. Su-Su was tall and thin with long, flaming red hair. She lived by her daily horoscope and planned to be an actress someday, which probably explained her talent for imitating other people's voices.

"Hello, welcome to Boy Talk. Thank you ever so much for ringing up," the message went. The tape would go on to explain how to leave a message after the beep or to punch 1 to hear all the messages other callers had recorded.

At four-thirty on the dot Crystal would very carefully remove the Boy Talk tape and put her father's back in, breathing a huge sigh of relief that nothing had slipped up.

"I can't believe how well everything is going," she said as she slipped the Boy Talk tape into the answering machine that day.

"Yeah," said Joni. "Especially after Su-Su did that cool imitation of April Mathis."

"I *was* pretty good, wasn't I?" asked Su-Su, grinning. "Well, I had to throw her off our trail. She kept bragging that she knew who was behind Boy Talk and that she was going to expose us. I just had to make my voice sound like hers and record a message saying that *she* was running Boy Talk."

Suddenly the telephone rang. Crystal's pulse began to race the way it always did when someone called in.

"Hello, welcome to Boy Talk ..." the tape began.
Beep.

"Hi, Boy Talk. This is Pulled in Two Directions, and I really need some help. I have this boyfriend I really like. I also have some girlfriends I really like, too. The problem is, my boyfriend and my girlfriends *hate* each other. Really! My girlfriends think my boyfriend is weird, and my boyfriend thinks my girlfriends are stuck up. I don't want to give up my boyfriend for my girlfriends. But I don't want to give up my girlfriends for my boyfriend, either. What should I do?"

Crystal frowned at the answering machine when Pulled in Two Directions finished recording her message. "I think that's awful," she said indignantly.

"Okay, 'Dear Abby,' you're always full of advice. What should she do?" asked Joni.

Crystal thought for a minute. She couldn't imagine Su-Su and Joni objecting to Evan. And she certainly had a hard time believing that Evan wouldn't like her friends. But if that ever did happen, she knew exactly what she'd do.

"I think her girlfriends just don't know him well enough," Crystal said finally. "And maybe he's jealous of the time she spends with her friends. She should try to get them all together so they could have a chance to see each other's good points."

"That sounds like pretty good advice to me," said Su-Su. "Why don't you call in and leave a message for her?"

Crystal nodded. "All right," she said. "I'll go into my room and use the other phone. I just hope no one recognizes my voice."

The instant Crystal stood up, the phone rang again.

"Rats!" she said. "Somebody's beating me to it."

Beep.

"Okay, you losers. This is April Mathis. Where do you get off imitating *my* voice on your stupid tape? That was so lame. I may not be one hundred percent positive who you jerks are yet, but I'm going to get even with you anyway. Listen up, Boy Talk!"

Crystal exchanged nervous glances with Joni and Su-Su and braced herself for the sound of the telephone receiver being slammed down on the other end of the line.

Nothing happened. The tape was silent.

"Maybe April's going to say something else," offered Su-Su.

"Well, I wish she'd hurry up so we can take some more calls," said Joni.

But the only sound was the continuing hum of the answering machine.

"Maybe there's something wrong with the machine," said Su-Su.

Crystal opened the lid of the tape compartment. It was still spinning as if it were recording a message. "It must be stuck or something," she told her friends. She flipped the switch to turn off the machine and picked up the receiver. "That's funny," she said, frowning.

"What's funny?" asked Joni.

"There's no dial tone," Crystal said. "It's as if April's still on the line or something."

"Let's call her house from your other phone and see if her line is busy," Su-Su suggested.

The girls hurried into Crystal's bedroom and looked up April's phone number in the school directory. Then Crystal dialed the number.

Blap-blap.

"It's busy!" said Crystal, holding the phone away from her ear.

"You know what *that* means, don't you?" Joni asked.

Crystal and Su-Su shook their heads.

"It means that as long as April called Boy Talk and doesn't hang up, we can't do anything to disconnect her," said Joni. "She's doing it on purpose."

"Oh no!" cried Crystal. "She said she was going to get even with us. That's exactly what she's doing."

Su-Su gulped. "Are you guys saying that no one else can call in to Boy Talk now?"

Joni nodded. "You've got it, Einstein."

Boy Talk was over for the day.

Chapter Two

On Sunday afternoon, Crystal, Su-Su, and Joni
spread out towels on the beach and plopped down
on their stomachs. They went to the beach almost
every weekend in the fall, before cold weather up
north sent tourists flocking to Sunshine Beach and
turning the whole place into a mob scene.

Brightly colored umbrellas dotted the sugar-fine
sand, and waves from the Gulf of Mexico lapped
gently at the shore. Seagulls strutted around searching for handouts. Crystal slathered on sunblock and
looked around for other kids they knew.

"There's Marissa Pauley and Megan Scully over
there, talking to Jordan Losen and Henry Ward," she
said, squinting in the direction of the lifeguard's
tower. "Do you think Megan likes one of them now

that you and Beau are back together, Joni?"

Joni looked up from the Lindsey Jones mystery she was reading and shrugged. "Megan's okay. It wasn't her fault that she got mixed up with Beau. I feel sort of sorry for her."

"So where is Beau today?" asked Su-Su.

"He went to Miami with his parents to see the Dolphins game," said Joni. Then she frowned and shaded her eyes. "Hey, look over there. Do you see that girl? I think her name's Karen or something. She keeps going back and forth between a group of girls and a guy who's by himself."

"So?" said Crystal.

"So maybe it's Pulled in Two Directions," Joni said.

Crystal gave the girl a closer look. "Yeah, you could be right."

"Hey, Crystal, check out who's coming," said Su-Su, sitting up straighter. With her tall, slim frame and her long red hair blowing in the breeze, she reminded Crystal of one of the red danger flags the lifeguards posted along the beach when it wasn't safe to swim.

Crystal followed Su-Su's gaze, and her heart did a double flip-flop. Evan Byrnes was sauntering across the beach. He was carrying his Windsurfer under one arm and its sail under the other. Alison Hamel was with him, lugging a beach bag and a boom box.

"Rats," Crystal muttered under her breath. "Can't he ever go *anywhere* without her?"

Slipping on her sunglasses so it wouldn't be obvious she was watching them, Crystal sighed as Alison skinned off her cover-up and began spreading a pair of beach towels on the sand.

Alison looked great in her aqua bathing suit. Her long blond hair glistened in the sun. It was so long that it brushed the chair whenever she sat down.

Shifting her gaze to Evan, Crystal sighed again. It was hard to imagine that she had lived next door to him her whole life and had only recently realized that she wanted them to be more than just friends— a lot more. She couldn't remember how many backyard cookouts their families had had together. All the times she and Evan had gone to Saturday matinees together when they were kids. And most incredible of all, how she had always thought of him as only a friend.

Evan was tall and wiry. He was constantly raking his brown hair back from his face, tucking the long strands behind his ears, and smiling his infectious smile. Every time he did it, Crystal's heart stopped. Like right now.

"Hey, Crys! How's it going?" Evan called.

Evan was the only person in the whole world who called her Crys, and the nickname was music to her ears. Before her crush on him, she could start a major conversation whenever he said hello. But now his smile and the way he said "Crys" turned her brain into tapioca pudding.

"Oh, um...hi, Evan," she managed to get out.

He was standing perfectly still and looking at her as if he expected her to say something else.

Suddenly Alison turned her icy blue eyes on Crystal.

Crystal felt her face turn red.

"Evan, are you going to stand there all day or what?" Alison asked irritably.

Evan shrugged. "See you around, Crys," he said and turned back to Alison.

"Why didn't you say something? You just sat there like a dummy!" scolded Joni.

"Did you hear him call me Crys?" she asked dreamily. "He's the only person in the entire world who calls me Crys."

"Gosh, no, we didn't know that," said Su-Su, faking innocence. "Get serious, Crystal. You've only told us that about a zillion times!"

Crystal threw Su-Su a grin. Then she stretched out on her stomach and pretended to leaf through a magazine, but her attention was really on Evan.

He hardly said anything to Alison while he brushed sand off his Windsurfer. Then he carried it to the edge of the water, unfurled the yellow-and-red-striped sail, and stuck the sail pole into the board. Pushing the board ahead of him, he waded into waist-deep water, turned the sail to catch the wind, and jumped aboard.

"Eeeek!" squealed Crystal, sitting up. She squinted as she watched Evan struggle to pull himself upright and hold the sail up at the same time. Seconds later, he was cutting through the waves like a pro.

"You knew he'd get up on the first try," Joni chided. "He always does."

Crystal sighed. "I know, but I can't help getting nervous when I watch him. It's so exciting."

She rested her chin on her fists and gazed out onto the water, where Evan was riding up and over the waves with ease. She tried to imagine what it would be like to be on the board with him, his arms locked around her protectively, surfing into the sunset.

Suddenly a voice behind her cut into her daydream. "If they think they're going to get away with this, they're in for a humongous surprise."

Crystal darted a glance at Joni and Su-Su. Joni's nose was still in her book, but Su-Su's eyebrows shot up, and she looked at Crystal in alarm.

It was April Mathis. Crystal's heart skipped a beat. Was she talking about Boy Talk? Had she seen the three of them lying there and said it loudly on purpose?

Then April spoke again, her voice even closer now. "Just wait until I get through with them," she said with a nasty laugh. She and Molly Triola headed for the water, passing within a couple of feet of where Crystal and her friends were lying.

"Now what is she up to?" asked Joni, who had surfaced from her book in time to catch the last of the conversation.

"I don't know, but I think she knows who we are," Crystal said nervously. "She sounded awfully confident."

"If you ask me, she's *obsessing*," grumbled Su-Su. "Why can't she just leave the whole thing alone?"

"Because she's April Mathis. She has to know everyone else's business and she's used to getting all the attention at school," Joni said. "She can't *stand* the competition Boy Talk is giving her."

Crystal nodded. "We've just got to be ready for whatever she does."

Just then another voice drifted across the sand. "Evan! Evan, can you hear me?" Alison was standing on tiptoes waving her towel in the air. "Evan Byrnes!"

When there was no response from Evan, who was windsurfing far out on the water, Alison frowned fiercely and put her hands on her hips. She watched until the wind shifted and Evan turned the board to run parallel with the shore.

"Evan! I'm getting tired of sitting here by myself!

Get out of the water!" she shouted.

"Boy, is she steamed," said Su-Su. "I guess he isn't paying enough attention to her."

"Alison's such a pain," muttered Crystal. "Evan has a perfect right to windsurf all he wants to. I hope he stays out there for a good long time."

But to her chagrin, Evan steered his Windsurfer to shore and hopped off, rolling up the sail and dragging the board across the sand toward Alison.

"Do you realize how long you've left me sitting here all by myself?" Alison demanded as soon as Evan got close enough to hear.

Crystal couldn't help feeling sorry for Evan. Alison was so *mean*.

Why can't he see her for what she really is? thought Crystal. *Why is he so blind to all her faults?*

She pretended to read her magazine as she watched Evan sit down on the towel beside Alison. The two of them began talking in low tones. Crystal could make out only a word here and there, but there was no doubt about it—he was apologizing!

Oh, Evan, she thought, her heart breaking. *If only you liked me instead of her!*

Chapter Three

Monday started as an ordinary school day for Crystal. She saw Evan once in the hall by himself and twice with Alison. Both times Alison had an angry look on her face.

"What does he *see* in her?" Crystal asked Su-Su and Joni as the three of them sat around Mr. Britton's desk after school, waiting for three-thirty to turn on the answering machine. "I just don't get it. She always looks like she's just been stung by a wasp. You'd think she'd smile once in a while. I sure would if I had Evan Byrnes for a boyfriend."

Su-Su shrugged. "You know what they say. Love is blind."

There were still a couple of minutes left until it was time to turn on the Boy Talk tape. Unable to sit still, Crystal got up and went over to the window.

She gazed out and focused on the sidewalk leading past her house. Evan was heading up it at a run.

"Hey, guys, Evan's home," she said in surprise. "That's funny. He always goes over to Alison's after school."

"Maybe she had to go to the dentist or something," said Joni.

"Maybe," murmured Crystal. She knew her friend was probably right, but she had a funny feeling in the pit of her stomach. She had gotten only a quick glimpse of Evan's face, but he had looked pretty upset.

The sudden ring of the phone startled her. She hadn't realized that Joni and Su-Su had turned on the answering machine until she heard the familiar Boy Talk greeting.

"Hello, welcome to Boy Talk . . ." the message began.

Beep.

"Hey, what happened last Friday?" asked a high-pitched voice. "I tried to call in to give Pulled in Two Directions some advice, but all I got was a busy signal for the rest of the hour."

Crystal, Su-Su, and Joni exchanged worried looks. How many Boy Talk calls had been lost when April tied up the line?

"Anyway, here goes," the voice continued. "If

you're listening, Pulled in Two Directions, this is Stand by Your Man. I think you should tell your girlfriends to buzz off and let you date whoever you want. I bet none of them has a boyfriend, and they're all just jealous. Who knows? Maybe one of them is trying to break you up so that she can steal your guy."

"That's terrible advice!" cried Crystal. "What's the matter with her, anyway? Pulled in Two Directions said she wanted to keep her boyfriend *and* her girlfriends."

"Well, you were getting ready to call in with your own advice on Friday, just before April pulled her stupid stunt," Joni pointed out. "Why don't you do it now?"

"What if somebody recognizes my voice?" Crystal asked. "I don't want to do anything to give us away to April."

"If she suspects you, she'd have to suspect everybody who calls in," Su-Su reminded her.

"I know, but—" The loud ring of the doorbell interrupted Crystal. "Who in the world could *that* be?" she asked, throwing up her hands in frustration.

"Oh, my gosh, I hope it's not your dad!" Su-Su said in alarm.

"He'd never ring the doorbell," Crystal called over her shoulder as she hurried down the stairs.

She stopped in front of the door to catch her

breath. *It's probably just the mailman with a package or something,* she thought.

She turned the knob and pulled the door slightly ajar to look out. Then she gasped in surprise.

It was Evan. His fists were jammed into the pockets of his jeans, and he had the saddest look on his face she had ever seen.

"Hi, Crys. Can I come in?" he asked, sounding miserable. He raked his hair away from his face, but this time he didn't smile.

"Sure, Evan, come on in," Crystal said. As she opened the door wider, her heart pounding, she darted a quick glance up the stairs toward her father's office. All was quiet.

"I hate to bother you," Evan began, "but we've been friends for a long time, and I need someone to talk to."

Crystal felt herself melting. Evan's big brown eyes were pleading like a lost puppy dog's. He needed her! How could she possibly say no?

Evan had been in Crystal's house hundreds of times, so he knew his way around. He headed for the living room sofa and sat down on one end.

Crystal perched on the other end and waited for him to speak. Her heart was hammering away like a woodpecker on a tree limb.

"Gosh, Crys, you understand people and always know the right thing to say," Evan began. "You're the only person who can help me right now."

"Oh, Evan, I'll do anything I can," Crystal said softly. Her heart was swelling into her throat as she reached forward and touched his hand. "What happened? What's wrong?"

"The worst thing that could possibly happen. Alison dumped me." He slumped against the sofa.

"Oh, Evan, I'm so—" She gulped and pushed hard to get the next word out: ". . . sorry."

"I should have seen it coming," Evan said. "Ned Jensen's been hanging around her a lot lately. I know he's popular and everything, but I trusted her. I never thought she'd . . ." His voice trailed off.

Crystal thought fast. She had to act sympathetic. That was what he had come over for. But another Crystal inside her was jumping up and down for joy.

She cleared her throat. "Gosh, Evan, you must feel awful. I mean, I never thought Alison would do a thing like that, either. Not to someone like you."

Crystal paused, then realized with a start that she was gazing at him with a love-struck expression. *Shape up!* she ordered herself.

Just then the shrill ring of the phone sounded in her father's office. Crystal nearly jumped out of her skin. Then she heard a voice say, "Hello, welcome to—"

"Maybe it's for the best," she blurted out, trying to talk over the sound of the answering machine. She didn't wait for Evan to reply. "I mean, maybe she's not the right girl for you."

His gaze flicked toward the stairs. "Have you got company?" he asked. "I didn't mean to interrupt anything. I can come back later."

"Oh, no," Crystal said quickly. "It's just—the radio. Let's get back to your problem. Maybe you're lucky that you found out about Alison now, before you got hurt any worse," she said over the frantic pounding of her heart. Had he heard the Boy Talk message? Did he have any idea what was going on upstairs?

If he did, he didn't let on. "No way," Evan said, shaking his head. "Alison definitely *is* the right girl for me. And that's why I have to ask you a major favor. I wouldn't ask it if I didn't know what a great friend you are, Crys. I mean it."

Everything was silent upstairs. In fact, the only sound in the house seemed to be Crystal's pulse pounding in her ears. She had a terrible feeling she wasn't going to like what Evan was going to ask. She could feel tears welling up behind her eyes.

"What do you want me to do?" she asked, giving him the most sympathetic smile she could.

A look of relief spread over Evan's face, and he raked his fingers through his hair and grinned at her. "Thanks, Crys, I knew I could count on you. It's pretty simple, really, but it means a lot to me. All I want you to do is talk to Alison for me and tell her that I still like her. And, Crys, would you do it real soon, like before school in the morning?" he added eagerly. "I've got to get her back before Jensen moves in on her."

Crystal stared at him, trying to keep her expression from changing. She knew that if she even blinked, her face would crumble into a million pieces and he would see the real feelings hidden behind her sympathetic smile.

"Well . . . I mean . . . I don't know her very well." Crystal fumbled over the words as she tried to keep her voice from shaking. *That's for sure,* she told herself silently. *And I don't want to get to know her any better, either.*

"That's okay," Evan insisted. "Alison knows you. I talk about you a lot. I've probably told her a hundred times what a great person you are. She'd listen to you, I know she would." He paused and his expression grew serious again. "You'll do it, won't you? As a friend?"

Somehow Crystal managed to nod yes.

Another grin appeared on Evan's face like magic. He jumped up, pulled Crystal to her feet, and gave her a kiss on the forehead.

"Thanks, Crys. Thanks loads!" he said and bounded out the door.

Chapter Four

Crystal stared at the door. Her forehead still tingled from Evan's kiss.

But it was only a friendship kiss, she thought sadly. He still wanted Alison for his girlfriend.

She trudged up the stairs. Evan had asked her the impossible. There was no way on earth she could help him get back together with Alison. But how could she break her promise to him? She needed her friends' advice.

Crystal burst through the door. "Guys, you won't—" She stopped dead in her tracks.

Su-Su and Joni were standing on either side of her father's desk, staring at the answering machine. The machine was silent except for the soft whir of the spinning tape.

"What's wrong?" she asked, walking over to the desk.

"April Mathis has struck again," Joni said between clenched teeth.

"She didn't even bother to say anything after the beep this time," said Su-Su, tossing her head in disgust. "But she has the line tied up, the same as Friday. She's putting Boy Talk out of business!"

"What else can go wrong?" wailed Crystal. "First Evan, and now this!"

"Oh my gosh, we forgot all about Evan," said Joni. "When you didn't come back upstairs right away, we peeked down to see what was going on. We saw Evan in your living room. What did he want?"

Crystal looked from Joni to Su-Su. Tears filled her eyes, threatening to spill down her cheeks.

"You're not going to believe this," she began in a shaky voice. "I can't believe it myself. Evan came over to tell me that Alison just broke up with him."

"That's incredible news," said Su-Su. "So why the sad face?"

"Well, that's the good news," replied Crystal. "Now listen to the bad news. He wants *me* to talk to Alison and get her to go back to him."

"What?" screeched Su-Su.

"You've got to be kidding," said Joni.

"I'm not," said Crystal. "He said he came to me

because I'm such a good friend—and he wants me to talk to her in the morning before school. I need help, guys. What am I going to do?"

"Well, what does your horoscope say?" asked Su-Su.

"My horoscope! Su-Su, this is serious!" cried Crystal.

"Of course it's serious," said Su-Su huffily. "What's Evan's sign?"

Crystal frowned. "How would I know?"

"You know when his birthday is, don't you?" asked Su-Su. She had picked up her backpack and was digging around inside.

"Sure, April twenty-fourth," said Crystal.

Su-Su pulled a well-worn paperback book from her backpack and began flipping through it. "April twenty-fourth, that's Taurus. And you're Cancer, right?" She didn't wait for Crystal to answer. "Cancer matches up romantically with Virgo, Pisces, and *Taurus!* I'll tell you what this says about Taurus."

"You and your astrology stuff," said Crystal, shaking her head.

Su-Su ignored her. "Taurus," she began. "For his good points, he's level-headed and always has his feet on the ground."

"That much is right," Crystal admitted.

"Listen up," commanded Su-Su. "Number two,

he's affectionate and loves to snuggle. Whoa!"

Crystal sighed. "You'd have to ask Alison about that."

"Number three," Su-Su went on, "he craves harmony and beauty."

Joni giggled. "Alison? Harmonious? Give me a break!"

"What else does it say?" asked Crystal. She didn't want to admit it, but she was beginning to like what she was hearing.

"We'll skip Taurus's bad points and get down to the section on how to make him yours," said Su-Su.

"Okay," said Crystal.

"Take him on a picnic to a beautiful place, show him some affection but be cool in public, and don't rush him into important decisions. That's it. Now you know exactly what to do."

"Sounds foolproof," said Joni.

"Oh, guys, you don't know what great friends you are," said Crystal. "I'll think of something to say to Alison tomorrow. But mostly I'm going to concentrate on Evan and do everything I'm supposed to do to interest a Taurus. He's my—" She paused and then finished dreamily: "my Dude in Distress! I'm going to be there for him and mend his broken heart. I'll convince him that I'm *much* better for him than Alison is, and he'll forget all about her and fall for me instead."

Chapter Five

"Has anyone figured out what to do about our little problem with April Mathis?" Joni asked when the three girls met at school the next morning.

"*Little* problem?" snorted Su-Su. She stuck her thumbs in the pockets of her patchwork vest and frowned. "If we don't get her off the line pretty soon, Boy Talk will be all over. Dead! Kaput! I just heard a couple of kids complaining about the Boy Talk line being busy when I got to school. Soon it won't even matter if April keeps tying up the line. Nobody will even remember Boy Talk ever existed."

"Fine, so what are we going to *do*?" Joni asked in exasperation. "We can't stop April from making a call from her own phone, and we can't force her to hang up."

Crystal was only half listening to her friends. She was keeping an eye peeled for Alison Hamel and worrying about what she would say to her when she saw her. She'd thought about it all last night, but she still hadn't decided what to do.

"There she is now," said Su-Su, pointing toward the school building.

Crystal quickly looked around, but Su-Su was pointing to April Mathis, not Alison Hamel.

Naturally April looked gorgeous. She was wearing a pale blue poet blouse with her stonewashed jeans, and she was deep in conversation with Kristin Murphy as they sauntered toward the school.

"They're probably talking about new ways of sabotaging Boy Talk," said Joni grimly. "They look as if they might be planning something big."

Just then Crystal felt a tap on her shoulder. Turning around in surprise, she came face-to-face with Alison Hamel. Crystal knew her mouth must be hanging open as she tried to compose herself.

"Eric French said you wanted to see me," Alison said, sounding annoyed. Her icy-blue eyes snapped with impatience. "Make it fast, okay? I have something important to do."

Crystal did a double take. *Eric French?* she thought. She shot a quizzical glance at her friends. Joni and Su-Su both shrugged hopelessly. Then Crystal remembered that Eric was a good friend of

Evan's. Evan had probably told Eric to say that so Alison wouldn't be suspicious.

"Oh, right," said Crystal. She hated being caught off guard, and she knew Alison could sense it.

"So what did you want?" Alison asked. She flipped her blond hair so that it fell in long waves over her left shoulder and waited for Crystal to reply.

I can't do this! a little voice inside Crystal's head cried. But she had to. She had promised Evan, and she couldn't go back on her word.

"I just wanted you to know that Evan really cares about you, and he's terribly hurt that you broke up with him," Crystal said in a rush. "I think you ought to reconsider how you feel about him."

Alison didn't answer at first. She just stood staring at Crystal with a disbelieving look on her face. Then she said, "If Evan put you up to this, you can tell him he's out of luck. I'm seeing Ned Jensen now." Whirling around, she marched away.

"Gee, there's nothing wishy-washy about her, is there?" asked Su-Su.

Crystal shaded her eyes with one hand and watched Alison head toward the school building. Her heart was doing flip-flops of joy. "I did it," she said, grinning broadly. "And she's definitely through with Evan. I've got to find him and tell him what she said."

"You'd better wipe that grin off your face," said

Joni. "You're supposed to be helping him out, remember?"

"Whoops!" said Crystal, covering up her mouth. "You know I really do feel bad that Evan's so upset. I guess I'll just have to do my best to make him feel better." With a wave to her friends, she headed off across the school grounds to find Evan.

She spotted him leaning against the bike rack. His arms were folded across his chest, and he had a grumpy look on his face. But the instant he saw her coming, his face lit up.

"Did you talk to her?" he asked eagerly. "What did she say?" He raked his hair back off his face and smiled at her as if he expected great news.

Crystal took a deep breath. This was going to be tougher than she had thought.

"I just talked to Alison a couple of minutes ago," she began. "And ... well, I have some bad news. Alison said she likes Ned Jensen. I'm sorry, Evan. I really tried."

Evan's smile drooped like a wilting flower, and his eyes filled with sadness. "Well, what *exactly* did she say, Crys? Did she actually mention Ned's name? I mean, maybe you misunderstood," he said pleadingly.

"No, I didn't misunderstand," Crystal said as gently as she could. "I think her exact words were 'I'm seeing Ned Jensen now.'"

Evan stared off into the distance. He clenched his teeth, and the vein in his temple started to throb.

"Okay, if that's the way she wants it," he muttered, sounding as if he were talking to himself. "I hope she and Ned have some great times together. I could care less. Girls are too much trouble. I'm off dating—forever!"

"Forever?" Crystal asked just above a whisper. *He can't mean* that, she thought.

"You've got it. *Forever!*" Evan said and stomped away.

Chapter Six

Crystal's heart broke into a million tiny pieces as she watched Evan walk away. *How could he possibly mean he was through with girls forever*, she wondered. She hurried back to tell her friends what had happened, tears brimming in her eyes.

"You should have seen the look on his face when he said it," Crystal said, sniffling. "And then he just walked off and left me standing there. I don't know how I'm ever going to be able to get close to him now."

"I'm sure he still likes you as a friend," offered Joni. "You guys have been buddies forever."

Su-Su nodded. "And if you're still friends, you still have a chance to make him see what an incredible girlfriend you'd be."

Crystal shook her head. She wanted to believe them, but she wasn't sure she could. Evan had made it perfectly clear that girls didn't interest him one bit anymore.

On the way to Crystal's house to set up Boy Talk after school, Joni made an announcement.

"I've figured out what to do about April," she said, smiling triumphantly. She was the only one of them who had ridden her bike to school that morning. Now the front wheel wobbled as she tried to pedal slowly enough to stay even with Crystal and Su-Su.

"What?" Crystal and Su-Su asked in unison, stopping.

Joni put on her brakes and stopped beside them. Her eyes sparkled with mischief. "Wait and see," she said. Then she pedaled off ahead of them, tossing a big grin over her shoulder.

Su-Su ran after Joni, her red hair flying out behind her. "Come on, Sparkman. Quit teasing and tell us."

"Nope!" said Joni, pedaling faster.

Joni still wasn't talking as the three of them got to work setting up the answering machine.

"You'll see in a couple of minutes," she said when Crystal asked for the dozenth time what her big plan was. Sometimes Joni drove her crazy.

At three twenty-five, Joni turned to Crystal. "Is your school directory still on the desk in your room? I need to make a call," she said.

"Sure," Crystal replied. "Who are you going to call?"

"Come with me and find out," Joni said mysteriously. "You too, Su-Su."

Crystal and Su-Su followed Joni out of Mr. Britton's office and across the hall to Crystal's room. Su-Su sat down on the floor, stretching her long legs out in front of her, but Crystal was too jittery to sit down. She couldn't imagine what Joni was about to do.

Joni picked up the Sunshine Beach Middle School directory and held it close to her so her friends couldn't see whose name she was looking up. Next she dialed a number and held the receiver out in front of her so that all three of them could listen.

The phone rang twice. Then a familiar voice on the other end said, "Hello."

April!

Crystal felt a huge grin spread over her face. Su-Su was grinning, too.

Joni put a finger to her lips for quiet and gently laid the telephone receiver on Crystal's desk.

Crystal could hardly keep from giggling out loud as she, Joni, and Su-Su tiptoed out of her room and closed the door behind them.

"Joni, you are seriously brilliant!" Su-Su cried when they were safely back in Mr. Britton's office. "You really gave it to April. Now we've got *her* line tied up, and she can't keep calls from coming in to Boy Talk!"

Joni smiled smugly. "Let's see how she likes not being able to use her phone."

A couple of minutes later, calls started pouring into Boy Talk.

Beep.

"I've got a problem with my boyfriend, and it's bugging me *big-time!* He keeps pictures of all his old girlfriends in his wallet! When I told him it made me jealous and asked him to take them out, he refused. He says they're just pictures. But it makes me wonder if he likes those girls better than me. Or if he's just planning to date me until our school pictures come out and he can get another trophy for his wallet! Just call me ... um ... well, Picture This!"

"I don't blame her for being steamed," said Joni after Picture This hung up.

Crystal sighed. "At least she has a boyfriend—one who still likes girls."

"But you have to admit, she has a right to be mad," said Su-Su.

"If Beau ever did that, I'd kill him," said Joni.

Crystal was too depressed to argue.

The Boy Talk phone rang again. *Beep.*

At first no one said anything, and the girls exchanged worried looks. Was it April? Had she found some way to break the connection? Or had she gone somewhere else to use the phone?

Then the caller came on. "I feel really silly doing this," said a girl's voice that definitely wasn't April's. "I mean, it feels weird. And you'll probably think my problem is stupid, but it bothers me *a lot.*"

There was a pause, as if the caller was getting up her courage. Then she went on, "I have this boyfriend, and I really like him. He's cute and popular, and everybody keeps telling me how lucky I am to be going out with him. But the trouble is ... I *hate* the way he kisses. I mean, he's just so *sloppy!*"

She paused again. "I'm afraid if I tell him, it will hurt his feelings. Or worse, he'll break up with me, and I don't want that. I just want him to learn how to kiss! What am I going to do? This is Kiss and Tell. Somebody please help me."

"Yuck! I'd hate going out with a boy who was a sloppy kisser," said Su-Su.

"Well, she'd just better stay away from Beau," said Joni, grinning. "He's the world's best kisser!"

Beep.

This time, instead of a voice, the girls heard the tape rewinding.

"It's just someone calling in to listen to the messages," said Joni, sounding disappointed.

"Maybe they'll have advice for Picture This and Kiss and Tell," said Crystal. "Their problems are *so trivial!* I can't believe they even called in with them."

Joni frowned. "What do you mean?"

"Well, Picture This should just buy her boyfriend an album and tell him to put his ex-girlfriends' pictures in it. And as for Kiss and Tell, why doesn't she drop some tiny little hints? Couldn't *she* show him how to kiss?"

"See? What did we tell you, Crystal?" said Su-Su. "You make a great 'Dear Abby' even when you're depressed."

Crystal sat in a chair beside her father's desk for the rest of the hour. She was only half listening to the calls that were coming in to Boy Talk. She just couldn't get Evan off her mind. No one else's problems could possibly be as bad as hers. No way.

Chapter Seven

Crystal stayed in her father's office for a while after Boy Talk was over for the day and her friends had gone home. She leaned against the window frame and gazed toward Evan's house. She wondered if he was there, and if he was, what he was doing.

"He's probably pining away over Alison," she told herself.

She sighed and thought again about all the good times she and Evan had had together, beginning when they were little. She kept remembering their trips to the beach to build sand castles and thinking about how they had loved to run splashing through the surf. Evan had taught her to ride her two-wheeler without the training wheels, although her father always thought he had done it. When her mother died, when Crystal was only six, Evan had brought her a single red rose from his mother's garden.

"And now he hates girls," Crystal said aloud. "That has to mean me, too."

Finally she managed to drag herself away from the window and head for the kitchen. She had to fix supper for herself and her dad. She definitely wasn't hungry, but this was her night to cook. Besides, she had promised her dad at breakfast that she would make spaghetti, a tossed salad, and garlic bread, his favorite meal.

She paused when she got to the kitchen and looked around the silent room. Sometimes she ached to have a mother around to talk with her about important things ... like boys. Especially at times like this, when she desperately needed advice on what to do about Evan. There were just some things a girl just couldn't share with her dad.

The only alternative was a stepmother. Crystal frowned as she pulled a pot out of the cabinet under the sink, filled it with water and set it on the stove. She couldn't imagine her father ever marrying again. And she definitely wasn't ready to share him with someone else, not even someone she could talk to about boys.

Soon the pasta water was heating on the stove, the bottled spaghetti sauce was simmering, and the garlic bread was wrapped in foil, waiting to be popped into the oven. Crystal was just tearing lettuce for the salad when she heard the hum of the garage door opener.

A moment later, Mr. Britton came through the door. "Hi, Sparkle. How was your day?" he asked, giving her a peck on the cheek.

"Hi, Dad," Crystal said softly. She loved it when he called her Sparkle, his favorite name for her. When she was three, she had stopped to stare at a sun-catcher in a store window. Her mother had told her it was made of crystal, just like her name. Crystal had jumped up and down for joy, pointing to herself and crying, "*Me* sparkle! *Me* sparkle!" The name had stuck. But right now, even hearing her pet name, she still had to work really hard to smile. "My day was okay. How was yours?"

"Not too bad," Mr. Britton said with a chuckle, "but I gave my freshman classes their first exam of the semester. I'll probably be in my office half the night grading papers."

Later, while they were cleaning up the kitchen after supper, Mr. Britton put an arm around Crystal's shoulders and said, "You seem a little blue tonight, sweetheart. Did something go wrong at school?"

Crystal shook her head and gave her father an appreciative smile. "I'm just a little tired," she said. She hated lying to her father, but this was just a teensy little lie. Besides, it would be hard to explain her feelings for Evan. Her dad liked Evan a lot, but as far as he knew, the two of them were just next-door neighbors and good friends.

Crystal went upstairs and tried to do her homework, but she couldn't concentrate. She sat at her desk and drew doodles on the outside of her notebook. Next she ran a finger over the letters CB + EB and remembered how only last week she'd joked with Su-Su and Joni about how her initials wouldn't change if she and Evan got married some day.

"Fat chance of *that* ever happening," she muttered.

Just then she heard the telephone ring on her father's private line. Startled, she wondered for an instant if she and her friends had removed the Boy Talk tape from his answering machine. They had, she was sure of it.

"Hello," her father's voice boomed from the other room.

There was a moment of silence, and then he spoke again. "Boy Talk? I'm afraid you have the wrong number."

Crystal instantly felt numb. She hadn't thought about the possibility of anyone calling after hours. Not when the time Boy Talk was on the line was listed so clearly on the flyer.

Who was that? she asked herself. Then a new fear almost choked off her breath. *Was it April, checking up on the number? What if she calls back and asks my father his name?*

Chapter Eight

The next morning, after downing a fast bowl of cereal and a glass of orange juice, Crystal said good-bye to her father and went to stand just inside the garage door. That way she could keep an eye on the front of Evan's house.

She'd had to choose between racing to school to tell Joni and Su-Su about the call to Boy Talk that her father had received last night or trying to catch Evan and walking with him to school.

Evan won out.

It had taken her ages to decide what to wear. She had plunged into her closet and pawed through the hangers, giving each outfit a quick look before eliminating it. Too old. Stain on the front. Bad color. And on and on until only two outfits were left. She slipped into her red miniskirt and a white ribbed knit sweater. Then she added a red oversized vest and stood back to admire herself.

"Definitely cool," she said out loud. She pasted a clown smile on her face and bounced her honey-colored curls. Instantly her smile fell. Her curls stopped bouncing. "Let's face it," she told herself, "I don't feel very cool today."

The other outfit matched her mood perfectly. It was a pale blue empire dress. She put it on and stood back to look in the mirror. The lace trim around the neck gave it a romantic look. Maybe, just *maybe*, Evan would see her that way, too.

Now, as she waited inside the garage door, Crystal glanced at her watch every couple of minutes. She began to worry as the hands marched steadily toward time for the bell. Where was Evan? Was he too broken up over Alison to even go to school today?

Finally the Byrnes' front door opened and Evan came out. Hoisting his backpack onto his shoulder, he trudged down the sidewalk. Crystal drew in her breath. The look of misery on his face was worse than it had been yesterday when she told him the bad news about Alison and Ned. It made her heart ache.

"Hi, Evan! Wait up," she called out, rushing toward him.

Evan stopped and glanced around. He swept his

hair back from his face, but his expression didn't change. "Oh, hi, Crys," he said.

"Want to walk together?" she asked, trying her best to sound like her old cheerful self.

"Sure." Evan shrugged and fell into step beside her, plodding along without saying another word.

Crystal's heart fluttered in her chest like a hummingbird's wings. So far, at least, her romantic outfit hadn't gotten through to him. Now was her big chance to let him know how much she cared. But she had to say exactly the right thing. It had to be perfect.

Looking up at him, she said softly, "You know, Evan, we've been friends for a long time. If you ever need somebody to talk to, I'm here."

A smile flickered on Evan's face. "Thanks, Crys. I know I can count on you. You've always been like a kid sister to me."

Kid sister! The words startled Crystal so much that she almost tripped over a crack in the sidewalk. Was that how he thought of her? As a stupid kid sister?

She was too hurt to respond. She kept her eyes down as Evan's words played over and over in her mind.

"I know I'll never get over Alison," he said sadly. "There's no way."

"Of course you will," Crystal said in a rush. "I mean, it might take some time, but you'll find someone else. There are lots of other girls in the world."

"Yeah? Like who?" Evan scoffed.

Crystal swallowed hard. She wanted to shout, *"What about me?"* But the words died in her throat.

"See?" Evan said triumphantly. "You can't even think of anyone. There will never be another girl like Alison. I mean, it's not just that she's pretty. Her personality is special, too. I've never met anyone like her before, and I never will again."

Crystal walked along in silence, her heart breaking all over again.

When they reached the school grounds, Evan stopped and turned toward her. "Hey, Crys, thanks for listening. I guess I needed to talk more than I thought. You're a real buddy." Then he chucked her gently under the chin and loped off toward his friends.

"What was *that* all about?" said Joni, coming up with Su-Su.

"Did you mend his broken heart? Did he finally discover you're his one and only true love?" Su-Su asked excitedly.

Crystal's eyes filled with tears. "No," she said miserably. "I offered him my shoulder to cry on, and he told me he'd never get over Alison. Then, as if that wasn't bad enough, he told me I'd always been like a kid sister to him. A *real buddy!*"

Su-Su gave a low whistle. "Bummer," she said.

"You know what *else* he said?" Crystal went on indignantly. "Alison is pretty, she has a great personality, and he'll never find anyone like her."

"You can say that again," said Joni. "Alison's cold and bossy. She's the total opposite of you."

"I know that!" Crystal exploded. She threw up her hands in defeat. "Maybe I should try to be more like her so he'd notice me. Obviously sweetness and sympathy aren't working."

"I don't think it would be a very good idea to be like Alison," said Joni, wrinkling her nose. "You might lose all your friends."

"Okay, then what?" demanded Crystal.

Su-Su shrugged. "Don't ask us. You've always been the one with all the good advice."

"Hey, I know," said Joni, her face brightening. "Why don't you call Boy Talk and get somebody else's opinion?"

Crystal gasped. *Boy Talk!* "Oh no! I forgot to tell you guys something really important! Last night my dad was in his office and I heard the phone ring on his private line. After he said hello, you'll never guess what he said next."

"What?" Su-Su and Joni asked in unison.

" 'Boy Talk? I'm afraid you have the wrong number.'"

Su-Su and Joni just stared at her for a minute.

"Was it April?" Joni asked finally.

Crystal shrugged. "I don't know," she said gravely. "But we may be in for a whole lot of trouble."

Chapter Nine

The more Crystal thought about calling Boy Talk with her own problem, the better she liked the idea. Every chance she got during social studies class that morning, she made notes in the back of her notebook about what she would say. The idea of going public with such a personal problem made her tingle all over. What if she messed up? Or what if someone recognized her voice? She would die of embarrassment!

First she had to find the right name for herself. It had to be something that fit her problem and didn't give her identity away.

Evan was Dude in Distress, but she knew she couldn't use that. Friends Forever might work, but she wanted to be more than friends. More Than Friends? Crystal wondered. No, that wasn't right either.

When the bell rang at the end of class, she headed for second-period English feeling very discouraged. She had written down and then scratched out tons of nicknames—Dudess in Distress, Damsel in Distress, Fair Maiden in Distress, Frustrated, to name just a few—but she hadn't made any real progress at all. There were only five periods left plus lunch. Then it would be time to place her call to Boy Talk.

"How does this sound?" she asked when she met Su-Su and Joni in the cafeteria for lunch. She had been scribbling again, and this time she thought she might have something. "Hi, Boy Talk, this is To the Rescue."

"Hey, that's a great name," said Su-Su.

"Yeah," said Joni, nodding. "I like it, too."

Crystal flashed them a nervous smile and went on reading. "I have a crush on a guy, but another girl broke his heart," she began. "I know I can help him mend it if I can only get him to really notice me. But we've been good friends for a long time, and he thinks of me as his kid sister. Not only that, he swore off dating forever. How can I rescue this dude in distress and make him think of me as a girlfriend?"

"Perfect!" cried Su-Su, clasping her hands

together. "It's beautiful. Crystal, when did you get to be such a great writer?"

"Do you really think it sounds okay?" asked Crystal doubtfully.

"It's awesome," Joni assured her.

"You don't think it gives my identity away, do you?" Crystal pressed. "I mean, lots of kids probably know that Evan and Alison broke up. He may have told a lot of people that he's never going out with anyone again. Somebody might put two and two together and think of me."

"Chill, Crystal," said Su-Su. "First of all, Sunshine Beach Middle School is a pretty big school. And second, how many people know about your crush on Evan?"

"Just you and Joni," Crystal admitted.

"Okay, then. What do you have to worry about?" asked Su-Su. "Nothing, right?"

Crystal nodded and closed her notebook. She pulled out her sandwich, but she didn't even take a bite. She was much too nervous to eat.

Crystal's hands were shaking so badly that it took three tries for her to get the Boy Talk tape into the answering machine that afternoon.

"Maybe I'll wait until tomorrow to call," she said. "I need more time to get up my nerve."

"Don't be silly," said Su-Su. "You've got a big problem and an incredible-sounding message. Why would you want to wait?"

"I agree," said Joni. "And who knows? By tomorrow Alison could be tired of Ned Jensen and want Evan back. I don't think you have any time to lose."

Crystal gulped. She hadn't even thought of that possibility.

"Okay," she said. "I'll do it today."

"Let's just hope that April won't tie up our line again," said Su-Su.

"Go ahead, call," Joni urged Crystal as soon as the tape was ready and the answering machine turned on.

"I'm … I'm still getting up my nerve," Crystal said. "Let someone else call in first. Then I'll go second."

"Chicken," said Su-Su. But her voice was drowned out by the ringing of the phone.

Beep.

"This is a message for Kiss and Tell. How can you stand to go out with a guy who's a sloppy kisser? That's so *gross!* I know what I'd do. I'd drop him before I *threw up!* Call me About to Barf. And I really am—just thinking about it!"

By the time About to Barf hung up, Su-Su and Joni were doubled over laughing. Crystal had to laugh, too. Soon she didn't feel so nervous anymore.

"I'll go next," she said. She grabbed the notebook with her message written in it and ran across the hall to her room.

She punched in the Boy Talk number and held her breath as she listened to the greeting. As soon as the beep sounded, she quickly read her message and hung up, hurrying back to the others.

"I did it! How did it sound?" she asked anxiously.

"Dahling, you were fabulous!" said Su-Su, striking a dramatic pose.

"No, seriously," Crystal insisted. "Did I do okay?"

"You were great," said Joni. "I'll bet this phone will be ringing off the wall real soon."

Crystal crossed her fingers. "I sure hope so."

She heard the tape rewind a couple of times. That meant someone had heard it. She chewed her lower lip as she stared at the answering machine, willing the phone to ring.

Finally it did.

Beep.

"Hi, I have a problem with my mom," said a girl's voice. "I know everyone's been calling in with romance questions, but I really do need help."

Crystal rolled her eyes and groaned. "Come on," she muttered, "*I'm* the one who need help. Get off the line!"

"I want to get my ears pierced, but my mom says no. She says I'm too young and that I don't need any more holes in my head. Can you believe it? All my friends have their ears pierced. But she says I have to wait until I'm sixteen! What can I do? This is Not Enough Holes in My Head."

Crystal let out an exasperated sigh and looked at her watch. There were only five more minutes of Boy Talk left for the day.

Then the phone rang again.

Beep.

"I've got some advice for To the Rescue about how to handle Dude in Distress."

Chapter Ten

Crystal hunched over the machine and held her breath.

"Take my advice and don't be a wimp," said the voice on the tape. "You have to guts up and go for it! He needs somebody strong to lean on now, and if it isn't you, it'll be somebody else. No matter what he says about being off girls forever, if you show him that he's been missing out on somebody special, he'll be all yours. Trust me, and just call me Gutsy."

The message clicked off and Crystal sank slowly into a chair. "Guts up and go for it?" she asked incredulously. "Did you hear that? What does she expect me to do? Call Evan up and ask him for a date?"

Su-Su had been staring at the answering machine

with a pensive expression. "You have to admit she has a point."

"*What?*" cried Crystal. "I could never do a thing like that!"

"Look at it this way," said Joni. "He's already talked to you as a friend about his breakup with Alison. You could make him think you're just offering him a shoulder to cry on again."

"Yeah," said Su-Su, grinning slyly. "And then when you've got him softened up, *bingo!*"

"Gu-*uys*," Crystal protested.

"Remember what my horoscope book said about winning over a Taurus?" Su-Su asked.

Crystal nodded. "Well, yeah. It said to invite him on a picnic to some beautiful and romantic spot, but I'd never have the nerve to do something like that. Besides, where would we go?"

"How about the beach?" asked Joni.

"At sunset," added Su-Su.

"Oh, sure," Crystal said sarcastically. "And what am I going to say to my dad? Dad, would you please drop Evan and me off at the beach so we can have a romantic sunset picnic? Get real! I'd die of embarrassment. Besides, what would Dad think?"

"You wouldn't have to say it exactly like that," said Joni.

"And don't forget, the book said Taurus is affectionate and loves to snuggle," Su-Su reminded her.

"Yeah, and there was one more thing," Crystal said, frowning. "It said be cool and don't rush him into important decisions."

"So what's the big deal? You're just asking him on a picnic," said Joni.

Crystal thought it over for a moment. What Joni and Su-Su were saying made some sense. And she had known Evan all her life. It wouldn't be as if she were asking out a perfect stranger. She wouldn't even have to make it sound like a date. So why was her heart pounding?

"What if he says no?" she asked, her voice just above a whisper.

"Remember what Gutsy said? *Guts up and go for it!*" said Su-Su.

"Oh, I don't know," Crystal said slowly. Then she had an incredible idea. "Joni, why don't you and Beau go with us? We could ask the guys for Saturday."

"Wow, that'd be cool," said Joni, nodding.

"What about me?" asked Su-Su. She stuck out her lower lip in an exaggerated pout.

"Oh, gosh, Su-Su. I didn't mean to leave you out," Crystal said quickly. "You can come along, too. If I tell Evan that all of us are going, maybe he won't suspect that it's sort of a date."

"So can I bring a guy?" asked Su-Su.

Crystal gazed at her friend in surprise. "Of course

you can. You know that. I just didn't realize you liked anyone right now."

"I'm only kidding," said Su-Su. "I have to baby-sit Saturday night. I don't know who I'd ask anyway."

"Well, Beau and I are definitely going," Joni said, "I'll call him tonight." She paused and gave Crystal a skeptical look. "But only if you don't chicken out. You call Evan, and if he says yes, you call me. *Then* I'll call Beau."

Little shivers ran up Crystal's back. *Why did I ever say I'd do this?* she wondered.

"Well?" Joni said, looking her straight in the eye.

"Okay, okay, I'll do it," Crystal promised.

Just then she heard a loud hum coming from the garage, which was directly beneath Mr. Britton's office. She gasped. "That's the garage door opening! Dad's home, and we're still in here!"

"Oh, my gosh! We have to take out the Boy Talk tape and put his back in!" said Su-Su. She fumbled with the little door to the tape compartment and yanked out the Boy Talk cassette.

Joni looked around for her own tape recorder, which held a copy of Mr. Britton's tape, while Crystal erased the Boy Talk greeting.

The garage door suddenly stopped humming. Crystal knew that any minute now her father would come into the house.

"Hurry, guys! We've got to make it look like no

one's been in here and then get to my room before he starts upstairs," she urged.

"The answering machine's ready," said Su-Su.

"Come on, then," Crystal said impatiently.

"Wait a minute, I have to find my books," replied Su-Su, spinning around in circles. "Does anybody know where I put them?"

The girls scrambled around the room, frantically searching for Su-Su's books. Finally Joni spotted them under a chair.

"There they are!" she cried, pointing.

Crystal scooped up the books. "Now let's get out of here!" she said. "We're going to get caught!"

They raced out of the room and across the hall, ducking into Crystal's room an instant before Mr. Britton started up the stairs.

"Hi, girls," he said cheerfully as he went past.

"Hi, Mr. Britton," Joni and Su-Su chorused.

"Hi, Dad," said Crystal.

"That was close," said Joni, breathing a sigh of relief as Mr. Britton entered his office.

Crystal closed the door to her room and leaned against it. "It was my fault," she said. "I guess I got carried away trying to decide what to do about Gutsy's advice." Then she had a horrible thought

What if they'd left something in her dad's office that could give Boy Talk away?

Chapter Eleven

Crystal paced her bedroom floor after her friends left. She had so many things to worry about. First, there was the naggy feeling that they'd left something in her dad's office. Then there was the even bigger problem: Not only had she promised Joni that she would call Evan tonight, but she had promised that she would do it as soon as Joni and Su-Su went home.

"What am I going to say?" she asked out loud.

She sat down at her desk and opened her notebook to the page where she had written her telephone message for Boy Talk. It had taken her half a day to get it just right.

But she didn't have half a day this time. *I've never asked a boy out before*, Crystal thought, beginning to panic. *How am I supposed to know what to say?*

She stared at the blank page of notebook paper until her father called her to supper.

"Hi, Sparkle," he said when she entered the kitchen. His white shirt was open at the collar, and his usually neatly combed hair was falling across his forehead. "I'm afraid it's only hot dogs tonight. I wish I could cook the way you can," he added, giving her a big grin. "You really take good care of me."

"You know I love hot dogs, Dad," Crystal said, smiling back. She couldn't help but feel proud. When her mother had died, she had been too young to cook or do anything else to help her dad out. But when she was older, she had worked hard to learn how to do all she could. She loved it when her father complimented her.

"Crystal, were you in my office this afternoon by any chance?"

Crystal froze. "Wh-what?" she stammered, trying to buy time. Maybe they *had* left something incriminating behind!

"The light was on when I got home," Mr. Britton went on. "I could have sworn I turned it off before I left this morning."

Relief flooded through Crystal. "Oh, that," she said, thinking fast. "I went in to sharpen a pencil. Guess I left it on. Sorry."

If her father noticed the shakiness in her voice, he

didn't let on. Instead, he asked about her day and made small talk about his own. It was the same kind of conversation they had every night.

When the kitchen was cleaned up, Crystal made the excuse that she had to do her homework and went back to her room.

It's now or never, she thought. *I've never had trouble talking to Evan before. I'll just have to wing it tonight.*

Evan answered the phone. "Hello?"

"Hi, Evan. It's me."

"Oh, hi, Crys."

She could hear the disappointment in his voice. He'd probably been hoping it was Alison.

Just stay cool and act normal, Crystal told herself, trying to ignore the butterflies zooming around in her stomach. "How's it going?" she asked softly.

Evan hesitated. "Okay, I guess. So what's up?"

Eeeek! thought Crystal. She hadn't planned to get around to the picnic invitation so early in the conversation. She had hoped they could talk awhile so she could ease into asking him to go to the beach.

"Um ... well ... I was just wondering." She fumbled for words. "Some of us are going to the beach late Saturday afternoon, and we're taking a picnic. We'd—I mean, I'd love for you to come along."

There was a long pause before Evan answered. "Gee, thanks, Crys. You're a terrific friend. But, well ... " His voice trailed off sadly.

Crystal gulped hard. Her pulse was racing. She had to get him to say yes, if it was the last thing she ever did.

"It's no big deal. Just a laid-back afternoon," she assured him. "Maybe we'll even stay to watch the sunset." She paused and crossed her fingers for luck. "And if you wanted to talk again ... you know, about ... things, well, I'd be there."

"I don't know," Evan said dejectedly. "I don't feel much like going anywhere. And the beach, well, Alison and I used to go there a lot. It would just remind me of her."

Crystal slapped her forehead with the heel of her hand. *Why didn't I think of that?* she scolded herself. *Now I've blown it—big time!*

But she had to make one more try. "Hey, the food will be good," she said, trying to sound as cheerful as she possibly could. "I was planning to make my famous killer brownies, and you know how much you like them."

To her amazement, she heard Evan chuckle. "Okay, okay," he said, "I'll go. Your killer brownies convinced me. And who knows, maybe I'll see Alison out there, and I'll get a chance to talk to her."

Crystal groaned to herself. *At least he's going,* she thought. *That's all that matters.* When she hung up, she didn't know whether to cry or be happy. Evan had agreed to go to the beach with her on Saturday, but not because he wanted to be with her. He just wanted to eat brownies and look for his ex.

Then she remembered what Gutsy had said. *Guts up and go for it.* That's exactly what she was doing. Maybe this was just a small victory, but it was definitely a step in the right direction. Once she got Evan to the beach, she would convince him that she was his one true love.

She reached for the phone again and called Joni.

"You're never going to believe this," she began as soon as Joni answered. "It took some talking, but Evan said he'd go to the beach with us on Saturday afternoon."

"Lucky you," Joni muttered.

Alarms went off in Crystal's head.

"I talked to Beau a few minutes ago, and I just happened to casually mention the picnic. And guess what? He already has plans. He's doing something with his obnoxious friends!"

Crystal stared at the phone. She knew she should say something sympathetic to Joni. After all, Joni and Beau had been having trouble over Beau's friends for a long time. But she couldn't get any words out.

She had told Evan there would be other kids along. And now she knew they would be alone. *She* would be with the boy she adored, while *he* was on the lookout for his ex!

Chapter Twelve

Crystal was crossing a street on her way to school the next morning when she heard someone running up the sidewalk behind her.

"Hey, Crys! Wait up!"

She stopped right in the middle of the street. There was no way in the world she wouldn't wait for Evan. So what if the light had just changed and traffic was whizzing around her?

"Hi," she said brightly as he dodged a truck and caught up with her in the intersection.

He raked back his hair and gave her the biggest smile she had seen since Alison dumped him. "Okay if I walk the rest of the way with you?"

"Sure," Crystal said. Her heart was doing little

flip-flops as the light changed again and they walked along together.

"Alison called last night!" he burst out. He spun around, walking backwards and grinning down at her.

Crystal's spirits took a sudden nosedive.

"She ... she did?" Crystal asked in a faltering voice. "What did she want?"

"Just to talk," said Evan. He turned around to walk forward again, but he was still grinning like crazy. "She said she was calling to see how I was getting along because she thought I looked bummed at school. She still likes Ned, but she's worried about me. Isn't that terrific?"

Crystal was dumbfounded. "What's so terrific about it if she still likes Ned Jensen?"

Evan shrugged. "Don't you see? If she's worried about me, it means she still cares. And *that* means she'll come back when she gets tired of Ned," he said. He sounded perfectly confident that it was going to happen.

Little bursts of anger flashed through Crystal. "You have to be brain-dead if you believe that," she said indignantly. "Alison is just stringing you along! Can't you see that?"

The instant the words were out, she regretted them. In fact, she hadn't realized that she'd said them out loud until she saw the hurt look on Evan's face.

"I'm sorry, Evan," she said quickly. "I guess I shouldn't have said that."

Evan shook his head. "I know you are just trying to help, but you're wrong about Alison," he said. "She's a terrific person, and I really believe we'll get back together someday. Anyway, I'm trying to hurry things up. I hope you won't mind, but I invited her along Saturday."

Crystal stopped dead in her tracks and stared at him. "What?"

"Well, you said there were a bunch of kids going. I didn't think one more would matter, and it would be the perfect chance to talk with her. Anyway, she said she'd have to think about it."

Keeping her eyes straight ahead, Crystal tried to keep the expression on her face from showing the panic that was growing inside her. Horrible thoughts were firing through her brain like shooting stars.

What if Alison says yes and comes along?

How will I explain why there's nobody else with us?

Will Alison figure out that I have a crush on Evan?

What if they get back together right in front of me?

"I'm going to take my board, anyway," Evan went on. "That way, if Alison doesn't go, at least I can windsurf. And eat killer brownies," he added with a quick grin in her direction.

Gutsy's words rang in Crystal's ears. If there was ever a time to guts up and go for it, it was now. She had to make a move, and make it *fast*.

"I'm dying to learn to windsurf," she blurted out. "I've watched you out on the waves, and it looks like a lot of fun. Do you think you could teach me?"

Evan looked surprised. "Cool," he said. "You're really interested in windsurfing? I mean, if Alison's not there, I could give you some lessons."

"That'd be great," Crystal said, putting all the sweetness into her voice that she could. "I'll definitely need help. It looks like it takes a lot of strength to pull up."

"Yeah, well, it does take some muscle." Evan straightened his shoulders and walked a little taller. "I'd probably have to ride the board with you the first few times and show you how it works."

"That's what I was thinking, too," Crystal said, nodding.

"You know, one thing I admire in a girl is guts," said Evan. "Alison and I used to fight about how she wouldn't ever do any sports. She was always too worried about working on her tan or getting her hair wet to try the board."

Crystal gave him her most flirtatious smile. Her heart wasn't just doing flip-flops now. It was doing triple-gainers off the high board. Gutsy had been right, and now she, Crystal, was really going to go for it. She would windsurf like a pro! She would swim all the way across the Gulf of Mexico if she had to! She'd do whatever it took to prove to Evan that she was the right girl for him.

When they reached the school Crystal said good-bye to Evan and glanced at the groups of students milling around the sidewalk. *Where are Joni and Su-Su?* she thought. Her friends both lived closer to the school than she did, so they usually got there first. Sometimes they waited for her by the front steps, but not today.

Crystal headed into the building and rushed through the crowded halls toward the seventh-grade lockers. "Alison's going to the beach with me and Evan on Saturday over my dead body!" she announced when she found Joni and Su-Su at Joni's locker.

Quickly she told them about her conversation with Evan on the way to school. "I'm really glad I followed Gutsy's advice. I'm going to keep following it even if it kills me!"

Joni had been checking out the mirror on her locker door, fluffing her short dark hair with her fingers. Now she turned and frowned at Crystal. "If Alison tells Evan yes, how are you going to stop her from going?"

"I don't know yet," Crystal admitted. "I'll think of something," she added with determination.

But deep inside, she wasn't so sure. If she found a way to stop Alison from going to the beach, would Evan refuse to go, too?

Chapter Thirteen

It didn't take Crystal long to decide what to do about Alison Hamel. She was leaving her own locker a few minutes later when she saw Alison a few feet away, deep in conversation with Hope Seymour and Ashley Malott.

She couldn't hear anything Alison was saying, but as she passed by she heard Hope say, "Gosh, Alison, it must be awesome having *two* boys crazy about you. I'm so jealous."

"Yeah," Ashley put in. "And both of them are so cute. I'd give anything to be you."

Crystal froze to the spot. She could hardly believe her ears. She had been right about Alison stringing Evan along. And now Alison was even bragging about it!

Crystal's heart was racing. The thought of Alison breaking Evan's heart and then using him to make herself look good in front of her friends infuriated her. How low could a person get?

Whirling around, she tapped Alison on the shoulder. "Alison Hamel, you are the most cruel and heartless person I've ever met! Where do you get off making someone as terrific as Evan think you still care about him? Is that your idea of fun? Why don't you just let him get over you and find another girlfriend? And if you think you're going to go to the beach with us on Saturday so you can wrap him around your little finger again, you've got another think coming!"

The other girls looked startled, but Alison turned her icy-blue eyes on Crystal and stared at her with contempt. Then she whipped her long blond hair over her shoulder and burst out laughing.

"Someone as terrific as Evan, huh? Don't tell me *you* have a crush on *him*." She turned to her friends. "His little next-door neighbor! Isn't that hysterical?" Then glancing back at Crystal, she sneered, "Worship him all you want to, kid. He doesn't even know you're alive."

Crystal felt heat blazing from her neck all the way up her face. She'd goofed up—big-time! Hope and Ashley were giggling along with Alison.

She wished she could die right there on the spot.

Desperately she tried to think of a great comeback. But her mind was blank. There was nothing to do but get out of there. Fast!

Crystal could hear Alison laughing all the way down the hall as she hurried away. She couldn't concentrate for the rest of the day. The awful scene played over and over in her mind. Why hadn't she just kept her mouth shut? Now Alison knew that Crystal had a crush on Evan. And she was just mean enough to tell him.

By the time school was out, Crystal was a total wreck. She told Joni and Su-Su what had happened, but they didn't have any great advice to offer. Only sympathy. Then they were interrupted when the first call of the day came in on Boy Talk.

Beep.

"Hi, this is Needs an Earful."

The caller paused, and there was giggling in the background.

"What's so funny about that?" asked Su-Su.

Crystal motioned for her to be quiet just as Needs an Earful spoke again.

"Yesterday I called in to hear the messages, and I only heard part of what To the Rescue said. I was wondering if she would call in and leave her message again. I think I might have some advice for her."

"You bet I'll call again," said Crystal. "I'm desperate! I'll take all the advice I can get." She jumped up and ran toward her room to make the call.

"Not so fast," said Joni. She ran after Crystal and grabbed her arm just before she reached the door.

Crystal looked at Joni in surprise. "What's wrong? Needs an Earful didn't get all of my message. I have to call in again."

Joni was frowning. "I don't like this," she said. "That voice sounded sort of familiar."

"It wasn't April, if that's what you're thinking," said Su-Su, coming up behind them. "I'd know her voice anywhere."

"Right," said Crystal impatiently. "So there's nothing to worry about."

"It might not have been April," said Joni, "but she could have had someone else call for her just to throw us off the track. Remember the first time she called? There was all that giggling in the background, just like today. I think April might have set this up to get you to call again so she can try to recognize your voice."

"Come on, Joni," Su-Su broke in. "I keep telling you, you read too many mysteries."

Joni flashed her an angry look. "That's why I've got the instincts of a detective. I can pick up on things neither one of you would ever notice. Let's see you do that with your horoscopes, Su-Su."

"Joni!" Crystal cried in exasperation. "The whole idea of calling in to Boy Talk is to get help. If Needs an Earful is nice enough to want to help, then believe me, I want her to have the chance."

Crystal was headed into her room again just as the phone in her father's office rang a second time. She stepped back into the hall to listen.

Beep.

"Boy Talk, this is Think Again, and I have a message for To the Rescue."

Crystal rushed into her father's office. "Maybe this is my lucky day after all," she told Joni and Su-Su. She pulled up the chair by the desk and plopped down, waiting anxiously for Think Again to go on.

"I listened to her problem about having a crush on a boy whose heart has been broken by another girl. She said he thinks of her as a kid sister, and she wanted to know how to get him to notice her and forget about his ex. Next, I heard Gutsy tell her to go for it. Well, I think To the Rescue would be crazy to follow Gutsy's advice."

Crystal was stunned. That was the last thing on earth she wanted to hear.

"Doesn't To the Rescue realize that if she makes a fool of herself trying to get Dude in Distress to fall for her, she'll probably blow their friendship, too? Then she won't have anything! No boyfriend and no good friend either."

Crystal's head began to spin. "Oh, no!" she whispered. "I *did* make a fool of myself!"

Even worse, Evan could find out about the fiasco with Alison. Alison would probably tell him herself. What would he think of her then?

"I'd die if Evan didn't want to be friends anymore." Crystal looked at Joni and Su-Su in bewilderment. "I thought I had everything all figured out. *Now* what am I going to do?"

Chapter Fourteen

After Think Again hung up Crystal thought the Boy Talk session would never end. Saturday was only two days away. She desperately wanted to concentrate on her own troubles instead of listening to other people's, but the phone kept ringing.

Beep.

"This is Not an Actress. I'm really confused. My best friend has just started dating my ex-boyfriend. I don't want to date him anymore, but I feel weird when I'm around them. We only broke up a couple of weeks ago, and I don't know how to act when he looks at her the way he used to look at me and things like that. I just stand there feeling stupid and out of place. What should I do?"

"If you ask me, it wasn't very cool of Not an

Actress's best friend and ex-boyfriend to start dating so soon," said Su-Su after the tape ended.

Joni rolled her eyes. "Tell me about it. I'd freak out if Beau and I broke up and he started dating one of you guys."

"Gu-*uys*," Crystal wailed. "How can you worry about Not an Actress when you know I need help? You heard Gutsy say I should go for it, and I did. Now Think Again comes on, saying I could wreck everything between Evan and me if I'm too pushy. What am I going to do now?"

"You're asking the wrong person," said Su-Su. "I haven't had a date in months."

"Well, maybe I really should call back in and leave my message so that Needs an Earful can put her two cents in. Maybe she's the only one who really knows what I should do," pleaded Crystal.

"Too late," chirped Joni. "There's only one minute left until four-thirty. Even if you put your message on, there wouldn't be time for her to call back in and hear it today. Besides, I've got an even better idea."

Crystal glared at her. "What?"

"Just as soon as we get the answering machine set up for your dad again, I think we should take today's tape into your room and play it on my tape recorder," Joni replied. "That way, maybe we can fig-

ure out who Needs an Earful is. If we think it's someone who's okay, then you can put your message on
tomorrow."

"I don't believe you, Joni Sparkman," said Crystal
in disgust. "I don't have all week, you know.
Tomorrow's Friday. What if I put my message on
again then and Needs an Earful isn't listening?
Maybe she'll give up if she doesn't hear it today. Or
maybe the phone line will be busy. Anything could
happen, and I'll miss the advice that could save my
life!"

Crystal knew she was being a little overdramatic,
but she didn't care. How could Joni be so stubborn?

"Crystal, I think Joni's right," said Su-Su. Her
usually sunny face was serious. "The more I think
about it, the more I have a feeling it was a trick, too.
I could disguise my voice and put your message on
for you, like I did before, but there isn't time right
now. We'll just have to wait until tomorrow."

Reluctantly Crystal agreed. She knew she was
being just as stubborn as Joni. Besides, April had
been awfully quiet the past couple of days. It made
sense that she might be at it again, trying a new way
to uncover their identities.

When Joni replayed the tape a few minutes later,
Crystal listened as hard as she could to Needs an
Earful's message.

Beep.

"I can't be sure if her voice sounds familiar or not," Crystal confessed.

"Me neither," said Su-Su.

"I'll play it again," said Joni.

She rewound the tape and they listened a second time.

"Well, it's definitely not April," said Su-Su. "She has a deeper voice than this girl."

Crystal closed her eyes and played the tape again in her mind. "I don't know if it's just because I've heard her message so many times, but she's beginning to sound familiar to me, too," she said. "I just wish I could figure out who she is."

"Think, everybody," ordered Joni. "This is important. Think about kids in your classes, kids who usually sit near us in the cafeteria, things like that."

Crystal went through her entire school day in her mind. She tried to remember who usually spoke up in class or had a locker near her or borrowed paper from her. Then she thought about April and her friends, trying to remember what their voices sounded like. But all the voices she knew were starting to blend together and sound alike in her mind. And now she couldn't even remember the sound of the voice on the tape!

"Oh, my gosh, guys!" Joni cried suddenly. "I know who it is!"

"Who?" Crystal and Su-Su cried in unison.

"Listen again and see if you don't think it's Molly Triola," said Joni.

She rewound the tape and played it for the third time.

Crystal's heart sank as she listened. Joni was right. The voice belonged to Molly, all right—April Mathis's best friend. The whole thing had been a conspiracy.

But the worst thing was no third caller with magic advice to solve her problem with Evan.

She would have to solve it on her own.

Chapter Fifteen

Crystal had just slipped into her sleep shirt and was sitting cross-legged on her bed polishing her fingernails a soft shade of pink when the phone rang. She knew her father was working late in his office again so she dove for it before it could ring a second time and disturb him.

"Hello?" she answered.

It was Evan. "Crys! Guess what? Alison just called and said she'll go!" Evan sounded ecstatic.

Crystal stared at the wall in disbelief. *No!* shrieked a voice inside her.

Evan didn't wait for a reply. His words were tumbling out. "She said she'd meet us there. I said late afternoon, probably around four. Was I right? Is that when you were planning to go?"

"Four's fine," said Crystal, fighting to keep her voice from quivering.

"She sounded great. And she even said she's really looking forward to a beach party," Evan rushed on nonstop. "If we get back together Saturday, I'll have you to thank, Crys."

After they hung up, Crystal stomped around her room, letting off steam. She grabbed her stuffed animals off the bed and pitched them one by one against the wall.

"Who does Alison think she is, anyway?" she shouted to the empty room. "She's doing this on purpose! She wants to show me that she can hurt Evan if she wants to, and I can't stop her. She'll probably wait until we're all together and then tell him what I said to her, too. I wouldn't put it past her. She's a creep! A loser! An industrial-strength *jerk!*"

Suddenly Crystal knelt and picked up her teddy bear. He was the oldest and dearest of her stuffed animals, and she hadn't meant to throw him like that. She hugged him close as tears blurred her vision.

Then another horrible thought popped into her mind. She froze, still clutching her bear. She'd forgotten that there would only be the three of them at the beach. Alone.

Crystal whipped into action. She raced to her desk and grabbed the phone, almost spilling the bottle of nail polish in her rush. First she called Su-Su.

"Su-Su, you've got to help me out. You've got to go to the beach with us Saturday."

Quickly she poured out the whole story. "Don't you see? It can't be Evan, me, and Alison. I'd die!"

"Have you talked to Joni?" Su-Su asked.

"Not yet, but I'm going to," promised Crystal.

"It'll mean canceling my babysitting job, but I'll do it," said Su-Su.

"Thanks, Su-Su. I knew I could count on you," said Crystal gratefully.

Next she called Joni and told her story again.

"Uh-oh. It sounds as if Alison is out to get somebody, and that somebody is you," Joni said soberly. "Evan must have mentioned your name when he asked her to go along to the beach party. So now that she knows you have a crush on him, she's going to play up to him and watch you squirm. I couldn't come up with a more evil plot myself."

"So will you come along? Please," Crystal begged.

"That will only make five people, counting Alison," said Joni.

"You're right," admitted Crystal. "We've got to have more bodies. Who can we ask?"

An instant later, she had the answer. "I know!" she shouted into the phone. "Beau and his friends!"

"Are you kidding? Those obnoxious jerks?" Joni said with a snort. "Only if you're dying to hear them belch 'Achy Breaky Heart'! I'm serious. It's the grossest thing I've ever heard."

"Joni, I'm desperate. I don't care if they belch 'The Star Spangled Banner' in three-part harmony," Crystal said. "I'll call Beau if you don't want to."

Joni was quiet for a moment. "Okay, I'll do it, even though Beau and I aren't getting along so well again. He still spends more time with those guys than he does with me." She sighed. "Anyway, I'll ask him. I'll tell him we're trying to get a big crowd together and to ask anyone else he can think of."

"Oh, Joni, you're the greatest!" Crystal said. "I'll hang up now so you can call him." She was just starting to put the receiver down when she thought of something else. "Joni, are you still there?"

"Yeah?"

"You can promise the guys some of my killer brownies, but tell them to bring their own sandwiches," she said sheepishly. "I know how those guys eat. I'd have get an advance on all my allowances for the next five years to feed all them."

"Okay," Joni said. "You've got it."

By the time school was dismissed on Friday, Crystal, Joni and Su-Su had recruited fifteen kids, and she was beginning to feel a little better.

"All I had to do was tell Beau about the brownies, and he jumped at the chance to come," said Joni as they headed for Crystal's house.

Crystal sighed.

"It may not turn out to be the romantic sunset picnic I was planning, but at least I won't have to watch Evan and Alison getting back together all by myself."

"Maybe she'll change her mind and not show up," Su-Su said hopefully.

"Oh, she'll show up, all right," said Joni darkly. "She wouldn't miss a chance like this."

"You don't think she's really planning to take Evan back, do you?" asked Crystal, stopping outside her front door. "She might do it just for spite now that she knows someone else likes him."

"Bummer," said Su-Su. "I hadn't thought about that."

"Me, neither," said Joni. "I sure hope not."

With a heavy heart Crystal led her friends inside and up the stairs. They had no sooner set up Boy Talk than the phone rang.

Beep.

"This is Needs an Earful again. In case To the Rescue didn't get my message to her yesterday, here goes again. I didn't hear all of your problem, To the Rescue, and I want to help. Would you please call in again? Thanks a lot. Bye."

"That was definitely Molly Triola," said Su-Su, twirling a strand of her long red hair and frowning at the machine.

"What are we going to do if she keeps bugging us?" asked Crystal.

"Ignore her," Joni advised. "And don't you dare let her hear your voice again."

"I could do my Whoopi Goldberg routine and tell her to buzz off," Su-Su said, grinning. "Or I could even do Bugs Bunny." She screwed up her face and pretended to chew on a carrot. "What's up, doc?"

Crystal couldn't help laughing. Then she got serious again and said, "Well, I can't do Whoopi Goldberg or Bugs Bunny, but I can make myself sound like a little girl. Wait here. I've got the perfect response to Needs an Earful."

While Su-Su and Joni looked after her in surprise, Crystal hurried to her room and called Boy Talk.

Beep.

"Hi, Boy Talk, this is To the Rescue's Little Sister," she said in a high little voice. She cupped her hand over her mouth to hold in a giggle. "She can't talk on the phone right now because she's with her new boyfriend. Guess what? She doesn't need your help anymore because Gutsy's advice really *worked!*"

Crystal could hear Su-Su and Joni laughing hysterically in her father's office. But Crystal wasn't laughing when she put down the phone.

She couldn't help wishing that what To the Rescue's Little Sister had just said was really true.

Chapter Sixteen

Crystal was up making brownies bright and early the next morning. She would need a ton of them to serve everybody who would be at the beach. She had already explained to her dad about the picnic and had told him that she'd agreed to bring brownies for the whole crowd.

Alison will probably turn her nose up at them because I made them, she thought miserably.

"You aren't taking *all* of those with you to the beach, are you?" Mr. Britton asked as Crystal pulled the third panful out of the oven. His eyes were glowing with mischief.

"You know I wouldn't do a thing like that," she replied. "Go ahead and try one. I need a taster to tell me if they came out all right."

Mr. Britton took a brownie off the platter on the counter and bit into it. "These are terrific," he said, taking another bite. "In fact, they may be the best you've ever made."

"You're just saying that so I'll leave more for you," Crystal teased. But secretly she hoped he was right, since Evan was going to eat them.

Don't be silly, she scolded herself. *You don't honestly think that your brownies will make Evan fall for you and forget about Alison, do you?* With a sigh, she measured another cup of flour into the mixing bowl.

After she had made four pans of brownies and sandwiches for herself and Evan, she went up to her room to get ready. She put on her favorite bathing suit, which was pale blue with cutouts on the sides, and brushed her honey-colored hair until it shone.

She couldn't help thinking about the picnic she had planned before Alison decided to spoil everything.

She had dreamed that Evan would take her hand and lead her into the water to teach her to windsurf. He would put his strong arms around her, and they would ride out across the waves together. And when they got tired of doing that, they would build a sand castle and maybe look for seashells. Later she would spread out the blanket and snuggle up close to him as the sun dropped into the Gulf of Mexico and turned the sky a flaming shade of red.

Crystal threw her hairbrush onto her dresser. *It would have been so romantic*, she thought angrily. *And Alison Hamel would have been history!*

Still fuming, she pulled on a pale blue cover-up that matched her bathing suit and gave herself a last once-over in the mirror.

"This is as good as it gets," she murmured and crossed her fingers for luck.

It took two trips to carry the cooler full of soft drinks and sandwiches, her beach bag, and the foil-covered platter of brownies over to Evan's house just before four. His father was driving them to the beach because Evan's board fit perfectly in the back of their Jeep Cherokee.

Crystal thought Evan looked a lot like his father, who was tall, thin, and handsome. He even raked his hair out of his eyes the same way Evan did.

When everything was loaded, they headed for the beach.

Evan and Crystal sat together in the backseat of the Cherokee.

"Okay if I snitch a brownie?" Evan asked. Grinning, he reached back with one hand and undid the foil around the tray of brownies just far enough to extract a fat brownie.

Crystal just smiled.

"Ummm, these are great!" Evan said. "I think I'll

eat them all myself." He finished off the brownie in two gigantic bites.

Crystal was glowing with happiness. Maybe the way to a man's heart was through his stomach after all. Still, she couldn't help noticing that Evan was constantly raking his fingers through his hair and fidgeting.

"I'm kind of nervous," he confided in a low voice. "I mean, what if she doesn't show?"

Crystal's moment of happiness faded instantly. Part of her hoped that Alison wouldn't show up. But she knew that that would only make things worse. Evan would be even more deeply hurt—if that was possible—and he would probably make good on his threat to stay girlfriendless forever. Either way, Crystal knew she would be the loser.

"She'll probably be there, since she said she would," Crystal murmured.

When they reached the part of the beach where the kids from their school usually hung out, Mr. Byrnes pulled up at the curb and helped them unload. "Just give me a call when you're ready to come home," he said pleasantly.

Crystal thanked him for the ride. Then she picked up her beach bag and the platter of brownies and trudged toward the sand. Evan grabbed the cooler in one hand, dragging his board along behind him with the other as he followed.

"Hey, guys. Over here!" Su-Su was yelling at them. She was standing on a beach towel and waving wildly.

Not that we wouldn't have noticed her anyway, Crystal thought, amused. With her flaming red hair and her iridescent orange bathing suit, Su-Su was hard to miss.

Joni was sitting beside Su-Su with a book in her lap. As Crystal and Evan headed across the sand in their direction, Crystal noticed that quite a few kids had already arrived. Alison wasn't among them.

Evan noticed that, too. "I don't see her anywhere," he said, sounding worried.

"It's only two minutes after four," said Crystal. "Maybe she wants to make a grand entrance."

She realized as soon as the words were out that she'd sounded catty, but Evan didn't seem to have heard her. He was too busy looking around the crowded beach for Alison.

They picked their way through the sunbathers until they reached their group of friends. Half a dozen girls sat on their towels watching Beau and Dan Turpin, whose nickname was Twister, toss a Frisbee back and forth. Living up to his name, Twister sprang up, grabbed the Frisbee, did a complete spin in the air, and sailed the bright green disk back to Beau just as he landed. Even Crystal had to be impressed.

"Hi, everybody," she called.

"Brownie alert!" shouted Marissa Pauley as Crystal and Evan found a patch of empty sand nearby and set down their things.

"Hey, not so fast," said Crystal, laughing. She held the platter over her head as hands grabbed for it from every direction. "I'll say when, okay?"

A few more kids wandered over during the next half-hour. Some slathered on suntan lotion and stretched out to catch the last rays of the day. Others ventured into the water. Evan sat beside his board, alternately looking back toward the street and staring at his watch. By four thirty-five Alison still was not there.

"Maybe she had trouble finding a ride," offered Crystal. She put a sympathetic hand on Evan's arm. He looked so sad it made her heart ache. If he had ever been a Dude in Distress, it was now.

Evan shrugged and started to reply, but something over Crystal's shoulder caught his attention. He looked surprised for an instant. Then his expression changed to horror.

"Oh no," he whispered.

Crystal's heart skipped a beat, and she turned around quickly.

Alison was heading across the sand toward them. But she wasn't alone. She was strutting along looking gorgeous—and holding Ned Jensen's hand.

Chapter Seventeen

"Hi, Evan," said Alison. She waved at him casually with her free hand as she and Ned went by. "Thanks for inviting us to the party. It looks like it's going to be fun." Then she spread out a couple of beach towels a few feet away and sat down, snuggling close to Ned.

Crystal saw Evan's jaw tighten. "Hi," he muttered. Then he turned his face away and knelt to brush sand off his board.

Crystal wanted to tell him everything was going to be okay because she was there. *But it doesn't matter to Evan that I'm here,* she thought helplessly. *The only person he cares about is Alison.*

Crystal glanced at Alison and Ned out of the corner of her eye. They were giggling and talking softly together as if no one else was on the beach.

They're disgusting, Crystal thought. How could Evan have ever gotten hung up on a girl like Alison in the first place?

"Crystal, come over here. We need to talk to you," called Joni. She and Su-Su were standing a little apart from the others. Both of them looked worried.

Crystal knew what they were going to say before Su-Su even opened her mouth.

"Who invited Ned?"

"Alison, who else?" Crystal said with disgust. "Poor Evan. He really thought they might get back together today. She's such a monster!"

"Uh-oh, don't look now," warned Joni. "Here comes the monster."

Crystal braced herself. She didn't know what Alison wanted, but she was definitely headed their way.

"Ned and I are starving. I hope you brought something to eat besides brownies," Alison said in a loud voice. "I never eat chocolate. It's bad for my complexion."

Crystal clenched her teeth. She wanted to shout at Alison that she should have brought her own food instead of freeloading, but she didn't. Evan had invited Alison. He probably forgot to say anything about bringing any food. Saying anything to her now would only embarrass him.

"I brought a bunch of ham sandwiches," she said, shrugging.

"Ham?" said Alison, wrinkling her nose. "Gross."

"Then I guess you're out of luck," Crystal snapped. She spun around and headed for the water.

Joni and Su-Su followed her.

"Why didn't you tell her to go home and make her own sandwiches?" demanded Su-Su.

"Yeah, who does she think she is, anyway?" asked Joni.

"I guess Evan forgot to tell her to bring something to eat," Crystal offered lamely.

"Oh, come on," said Su-Su. "Alison's smart enough to figure that out. I think she just wants to see how much she can get away with."

"I agree," Joni said emphatically.

"You're probably right," said Crystal with a sigh. *And Alison's probably laughing her head off, too,* she added to herself.

She shaded her eyes with one hand and squinted toward the rest of the kids. A few had set up a makeshift volleyball net and were playing a game, but most were still sunbathing.

It took her a moment to find Evan. He was sitting on a beach towel talking to Marissa Pauley and Dawn Norgren. Crystal's stomach lurched. Why was he talking to them instead of her? Then she realized that Marissa and Dawn's towel was only a few feet from Alison and Ned's. Evan was talking and laughing as if he were having the time of his life.

He's faking it for Alison's benefit, she thought sadly. *Poor Evan.*

She tucked a strand of hair behind her ear and watched him a few minutes longer. Alison wasn't paying the slightest bit of attention to Evan. Crystal's heart was filled with pity. Suddenly she couldn't stand it any longer.

"I'll see you guys later," she told Joni and Su-Su. "It's Crystal to the rescue! I'm going after my dude in distress!"

"Way to go!" Su-Su called out after her.

"Good luck," Joni chimed in.

Crystal rushed up the sand and sank to her knees beside Evan. "Hi, Marissa. Hi, Dawn. Hey, Evan, sorry to tear you away from such gorgeous company"—she gave Marissa and Dawn a quick grin—"but you promised you'd teach me to windsurf, remember?"

Evan looked surprised. He didn't say anything for a moment. She could see the muscles in his jaw tighten again as he flicked a quick glance toward Alison and Ned.

Then he smiled at Crystal. "What are we waiting for?"

She helped him drag the board into waist-deep surf and unfurl the sail. Next, Evan spread the sail out on the water and tipped the board sideways until he could fit the sail pole into a hole in the center of the board.

"There's a trick to getting up," he explained. "Watch."

Evan grabbed the bar across the sail and at the same time hopped onto the edge of the board. He leaned backward to pull up the sail and shifted to keep his balance at the same time. Instantly a breeze filled the sail, and he was gliding out across the water.

"*I'm* going to do that?" shouted Crystal.

"Sure," Evan said, giving her a wave. "There's nothing to it."

Crystal took a deep breath and let it out slowly as she waved back. *Why did I ever tell him I wanted to windsurf?*

Deep down she knew why. Evan had said that he liked girls who tried new things, and that he and Alison had fought over the fact that all she wanted to do at the beach was sunbathe.

Crystal glanced around. Alison and Ned were watching her. Squaring her shoulders, she turned back to look at Evan. She was going to do this. It was now or never.

Evan rode the board out a little way and then came back, hopping off beside her and letting down the sail.

"This time you climb on while I hold the board steady," he said. "Grab the bar and give me room. I'll stand in back of you. It's really pretty easy."

"Easy for you to say," Crystal said lightly. She hoped he couldn't see how nervous she was.

"Ready?"

She nodded before she could lose her nerve.

Evan held on to the Windsurfer as she scrambled aboard. The board tilted crazily as he climbed on, but he caught the bar and kept it upright. He reached around her from both sides and grabbed the bar next to her hands.

Crystal felt a flush come over her as she felt his arms around her for the very first time since he used to chase her and kiss her when they were three.

Suddenly the wind shifted, catching the sail, and the board tilted again. Evan tried to keep it upright, but they both lost their balance. Arms and legs went every which way as Crystal plunged into the water, landing on top of Evan.

She went under and came up sputtering.

Evan was standing beside the board, shaking the water out of his hair. He burst out laughing when he saw her. "Hey, you look like a drowned rat!"

Crystal lunged for him. "I'm not drowned yet!" she shouted. Then she jumped on him and pushed his head underwater.

He came up an instant later and grabbed for her,

but she was too quick. She ran through the waves to the beach, turned around, and stuck her tongue out at him.

"Get back down here and try this board again or you're a chicken," he called.

"Are you daring me?" she challenged.

Evan chuckled. "Sure, come on."

Crystal hurried back into the water. Learning to ride the board was fun, after all. She couldn't wait to try it again. And she didn't even care what Alison thought anymore.

It took two more tries for her to get her timing right, hopping onto the board at the same time Evan pulled himself up.

"Hang on!" he said in her ear.

Suddenly the wind filled the sail and they were skimming over the waves, laughing seagulls wheeling overhead.

Crystal held on tightly, wishing the moment would last forever.

Chapter Eighteen

Over and over they rode the board. Slowly the current began to pull them down the beach and away from their friends.

This windsurfing business was getting easier for Crystal. A couple of times she took a turn by herself, but she liked it best when she and Evan sailed across the sparkling water together, his arms encircling her.

Finally they both began to get tired.

"What do you say we take a break?" Evan asked as they beached the board.

"Okay with me," said Crystal. "I'm beat. Even my toes are tired from gripping that board."

"We're pretty far down from where we started," said Evan. "Why don't we sit down here for a few minutes before we head back?"

Crystal glanced down the beach and smiled when she saw how far they were from the others. At last she was alone with Evan.

A tingle raced up her spine. "Okay," she said.

Evan stretched out on his stomach, propping himself up on his elbows.

Crystal sat down beside him. Even though she was tired, she was still bubbling with excitement. "I'm so glad you took me out there. I was a little nervous at first, but once I got the hang of it, it was easy."

Evan didn't answer. He was staring out at the water, and the muscle in his jaw was tightening again.

"I don't know how I could have been so stupid," he snapped.

Crystal suddenly realized he hadn't heard anything she had just said.

"I should have known she'd bring Jensen with her. She told me she over the phone how crazy she was about him."

Crystal looked down at the sand, feeling as though her heart would burst. She had been having so much fun that she'd convinced herself Evan was having fun, too. *And* that he wasn't thinking about Alison anymore. But he had been, of course. All the time he was laughing and teasing her and teaching her to windsurf, he'd had Alison on his mind.

"I'm really sorry..." Her voice trailed off. She

couldn't think of anything else to say.

"She won't get the chance to make a fool of me again. You can count on that," Evan said angrily. "I said I was off girls forever. Well, I am! All of them! Especially her! I wouldn't take her back now even if she begged me."

Crystal tried to swallow the lump in her throat. But it wouldn't go away. And it was growing bigger and bigger. Tears brimmed in her eyes and threatened to spill down her cheeks.

"You don't really mean you're off girls forever, do you?" she asked softly. "I mean, not *all* girls, *forever?*"

"That's exactly what I mean," he said emphatically. "No girl's ever going to get a chance to do this to me again."

Crystal bit her bottom lip and thought about the two messages she had gotten on Boy Talk. Gutsy had said to go for it, but Think Again had warned her to be careful or she would lose him completely.

But I'm already losing him, she thought miserably.

Taking a deep breath, she plunged ahead. "But if you stop dating, that will be a victory for Alison. Don't you see? Her ego will go straight through the roof."

"Who cares?" Evan grumbled. "Alison can think whatever she wants to."

Crystal let a moment of silence go by. She had an

idea, but she didn't know if Evan would go for it. Still, she thought, what did she have to lose?

"Why don't you just hang around with me for a while? I mean, we're friends and everything. And you know you can talk to me. That way you'd fake out Alison."

He gave her a puzzled look. "What are you talking about? Make her think you and I are going out?"

"Um ... sort of. Actually, she could think whatever she wants to, like you said. At least she wouldn't think you're pining away for her."

Evan seemed to be thinking it over. "What about your friends? You don't mean hang around with all three of you, do you? You guys are pretty tight."

"No, silly." Crystal told him, her heart pounding. "Just you and me. It might be fun."

"Yeah, but what would you tell Joni and Su-Su to keep them from getting mad?" he asked.

She grinned slyly. "That's easy. I'll just tell them we're going out."

Evan shook his head and chuckled softly. "You know something? It's funny you said that. There were a couple of times before I started going with Alison that I wanted to ask you out."

Crystal gulped. "You did? Well, why didn't you?" she asked, feeling breathless.

Evan shrugged. "Oh, you know. We grew up together. I guess I thought that since we were always such good friends, I'd wreck everything if I asked you out."

Crystal couldn't believe her ears. This was crazy! It was unbelievable! It was too wonderful to be true! She wanted more than anything to jump up and kiss him!

But something stopped her just in time. It was Think Again's warning, creeping back into her thoughts. If she got carried away now, she might scare him off. She couldn't risk that. Not when everything was suddenly starting to work!

"Promise you won't think I'm silly," she began slowly, "but there have been times when I wanted to go out with you, too."

Evan stared at her. "You're kidding."

"No, I'm not," she said softly.

"You're not just telling me that to make me feel better, are you, Crys?"

"No, honest," said Crystal. "I was just afraid to let you know before how I felt, especially after you said I was like a kid sister to you. You called me a *real buddy!* And then Alison ..." Her voice trailed away. She couldn't say anymore.

"Let me get this straight." Evan shook his head as if he were trying to understand. "We both wanted to go out with each other. But we both thought the other person only thought of us as friends."

Crystal nodded slowly.

Evan stared at her as if he was still trying to figure things out. Suddenly he started to chuckle. "So what changed your mind about me?"

"What do you mean?" Crystal asked.

"You used to cry when I kissed you. Remember? Back when we were little kids, and I used to chase you around the backyard?" he asked.

Crystal felt herself blush. "You remember that?" she asked, her voice a tiny whisper.

"Sure," he said, giving her a silly grin. "But no matter how many times you cried, I kept on trying."

Crystal hid her face. It was true. Evan had tried to kiss her dozens of times. And best of all, he hadn't forgotten.

"Well, maybe we should give it a try—just as friends, I mean," he said softly. "You know, to see how it goes."

Crystal felt a stab of disappointment. Why had he brought up kissing her if he only wanted to be friends? Still, she couldn't pass up this chance to show him that they were perfect for each other. And maybe he was just as nervous as she was about changing their friendship into a romance.

"Maybe we should give it a try," she said finally.

"Okay, great. Do you want to go to a movie this weekend?" he asked.

"I'd love to," she replied.

Her whole body was tingling with happiness.

Everything was going to work out fine. Evan wasn't a dude in distress anymore. He had finally seen Alison for what she really was, and he had found the girl who was meant for him, even if ne didn't totally realize it yet.

He will! she thought and smiled to herself.

"Hey, I thought this was supposed to be a picnic. Isn't it time to eat yet?" Evan asked, jumping to his feet.

"It sure is," she said. "We'd better be getting back."

The two of them started down the beach. Evan pulled the board along behind him with one hand and, after a moment, took Crystal's hand in the other.

At the instant their hands touched the sky turned an incredible shade of red as the fiery sun began to sink slowly into the sea. Pink cotton-candy clouds floated above the two of them, and soft waves lapped the shore as they walked along.

Thanks, Boy Talk, Crystal thought happily. *And thanks, Gutsy and Think Again—whoever you are.*

Hi, guys! This is Crystal. Hope you liked Dude in Distress. *Here's a sneak peek at Book #3:* Too Many Guys

Su-Su twirled a strand of red hair around one finger and listened as Too Many Guys went on.

"I know it was wrong to accept two dates," the caller said. "But I've come up with an idea to make it okay. I really do like the first boy as a friend and I don't want to hurt him by breaking the date, so I've decided to fix him up with someone else. But the girl who goes out with him has to be the perfect girl for him."

"I'll tell you a little bit about him. He's really tall with wavy dark hair and these totally gorgeous eyes. He has a great personality and he's really fun to be with."

Wow! Su-Su thought. This guy sounded too good to be true.

"Anyway, any girl who is interested can call Boy Talk and talk about herself. I'll listen to all the recordings, and choose the ones I think sound best. Come on, all you great girls out there. This is your big chance!"

WRITE TO "DEAR BOY TALK"

NEED ADVICE ABOUT

DATING?   **FRIENDSHIP?**   **ROMANCE?**

Joni, Crystal, and Su-Su may have an answer for you!

Just write to *Dear Boy Talk* at this address:

 Random House, Inc.
201 East 50th Street
New York, NY 10022

Attn: "Dear Boy Talk"
28th Floor

Let us know what's on your mind. From secret crushes to broken hearts to major embarrassments, Boy Talk™ can help! We can't publish every letter, but we can promise to print a select few in the back of every new Boy Talk book.

Too shy to share your romance problems? Boy Talk fans can give advice for readers' problems, too! Letters will begin appearing in Boy Talk #2: DUDE IN DISTRESS. Just pick a problem and write to the above address— and you just might see *your* letter in print!

And here's the best part: Everybody who writes to Dear Boy Talk will get—absolutely free!—

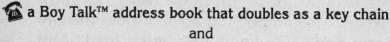 a Boy Talk™ address book that doubles as a key chain
and
a prepaid calling card good for five free minutes of phone time to any number in the U.S.*

So don't put your romance on hold—
write to Dear Boy Talk today!

*Offer good while supplies last. Please allow 6 weeks for delivery.

Dear Boy Talk,
My parents hate my boyfriend. So I started going out with a guy they _do_ like, too, so they won't think I'm going steady with the first guy. Anyway, there's going to be a formal dance at school and I want to go with my real boyfriend. But my parents want me to go with the one I don't like. What do I do now?

Two-Faced
Massachusetts

Dear Two-Faced,
You like to live dangerously, don't you? My first question is: Do these two guys know about each other? And second: Does the guy you don't like know he's being used? And third: How does your real boyfriend feel about you going out with the other guy? It seems to me you should rethink this whole thing before it backfires and you don't have _any_ boyfriend.

Joni

Dear Two-Faced,
I can sympathize that you'd do almost anything to keep the boyfriend you really love. I also know that parents don't always see our friends and boyfriends for who they really are. Maybe you should invite your real boyfriend over for a cookout or something so that your parents can get to know him better and see all his good points. Maybe then they'd let you go to the dance with him. Good luck. I hope it works.

Crystal

Dear Two-Faced,
I sort of agree with Crystal, except that if the boy you like knows your parents hate him, he probably wouldn't show up for any cookout. What do you think of this plan of action? I think you should get a bunch of your friends to take turns dropping by your house when your parents are home so they can talk about what a fabulous person he is. They could say things like, "He's the nicest guy in our school"; "He gets a lot of respect"; "The teachers all think he's terrific." Things like that. They would be talking to you, of course, but if you worked it right, your parents would have to overhear and realize they'd been wrong about him. They'd probably even want him to be your date for the dance. Go for it!

Su-Su

Dear Boy Talk,
My friend is having a slumber party and she's inviting some guys that we all hang out with. It's okay with her parents because the guys will sleep in the family room. None of the guys are our boyfriends, except I like one of them. The problem is, my mother won't let me go if I tell her boys will be there. I'm scared she'll find out. What should I do? I really want to go.

Sleepless in St. Louis
Missouri

Dear Sleepless,
Does that ever sound romantic. I'd never get to sleep if I knew the boy I liked was under the same roof! But if your friend's parents think it's okay, maybe her mom could talk to your mom and explain the separate sleeping arrangements and how they'll be in the house and everything. Once your mom understands, she'll probably let you go. Just don't let on to her that you like one of the guys!

Crystal

Dear Sleepless,
Believe me, I know what it's like to have an overprotective mother! Mine thinks every time I go out the front door someone's going to grab me. I wish I knew what to tell you, but I don't. If I *did* know, I'd do it myself!

Su-Su

Dear Sleepless,
I agree with Crystal about having your friend's mother talk to your mother, but I'd go further than that. I'd make sure your mother trusts you to do the right thing. As long as she knows she can depend on you in tough situations, she won't worry so much. Have a talk with her and let her see how mature you are. You are mature, aren't you? (Just kidding.)

Joni

Dear Boy Talk,
I used to love my boyfriend a lot, but I don't anymore. How can I tell him without hurting his feelings? I still like him as a friend, and I know he loves me a lot.

> Break-up Wimp
> Michigan

Dear Wimp,
Let's face it, you can't. If he really likes you, he's going to be hurt. But you owe it to him to be honest and not string him along.

Joni

Dear Wimp,
My suggestion for you is to tell him first, before you breathe a word about how you feel to your friends. He would be twice as hurt if he heard it from someone else, and if you still like him as a friend, you have to care about his feelings.

Crystal

Dear Wimp,
Why break up with him at all? You don't have to be madly in love with someone to go out and have a good time. What's the alternative? Sitting home and wishing you had a date? Just think of all the girls out there who don't have boyfriends and would gladly trade places with you—like me.

Su-Su

Dear Boy Talk,
I am totally into horoscopes and stuff. So I met this cute guy the other day, and he seemed totally perfect! We hit if off right away. Then I found out he was born in June, so he's a Gemini. My sign is Cancer and those two signs don't get along. My book says constant friction is in the stars, whatever that means. What should I do? Should I still go out with him?

Not My Sign
California

Dear Not,
A cute guy? A Gemini? That's my sign! If you don't want him, send him my way! Ha! Seriously, though, horoscopes don't lie. More people could save themselves a lot of grief if they believed what the stars told them. I'd hate to see you ruin a perfectly good romance by fighting all the time. You'd be better off to pass on this guy.

Su-Su

Dear Not,
Get serious. You don't honestly believe all that stuff about Venus and Mars lining up to rule your life, do you? I mean, if the planets are in control, why bother getting up in the morning? Use your head. If he seems totally perfect and you two hit it off, give it a chance! It could be the greatest thing that ever happened!

Joni

Dear Not,
I'm not sure how I feel about horoscopes.
I mean, sometimes they really seem to
come true. But other times I'm glad they
don't. Back to your problem, I think it
would be worth it to go out with him at
least once and see how you get along and
how much you have in common. It's hard
to fight with someone when you agree on
lots of things. And don't forget, sometimes making up after a big argument is
so sweet, it makes it all worthwhile.

Crystal

Dear Boy Talk,
My boyfriend is so gross! I mean, he's cute and super
nice but sometimes he can act so disgusting! He thinks
it's really funny to burp out loud and make vile noises
with his armpit (along with other gross stuff that I
won't even tell you about!). I've told him that I don't
think stuff like that is funny, but he does it anyhow.
This is so embarrassing—especially when my friends are
around. I can't stand it anymore . . . please help!
                    Grossed Out in Tennessee

Dear Grossed Out,
Boy, do I ever understand your problem. My boyfriend Beau acts disgusting sometimes, too, especially when his friends are around. I get the feeling they're having a contest to see who's the most obnoxious! We've gone round and round about this, and I finally decided that sometimes guys are afraid other guys will think they're sissies if they don't show off and act like baboons. I guess it's a guy thing. What can I say? You'll probably just have to hang in there and hope he grows up.

Joni

Dear Grossed Out,
I say give him a dose of his own medicine. Act giggly and silly around his friends. See how he likes that. And if he says something to you about it, remind him of his own behavior. He'll get the message—unless of course he's a total jerk. Then who cares?

Su-Su

Dear Grossed Out,
Su-Su is one of my best friends, but I don't know how she can say a thing like that. I'd rather die than make a fool of myself in front of my boyfriend and embarrass both of us in front of his friends. There has to be a better way to make him understand how you feel. Try having a very serious talk with him. And maybe throw in a couple of tears. Boys can't stand to see girls cry! And if he really cares for you, he'll change.

Crystal

Dear Boy Talk,
Help! Every day after school, I play basketball with the same group of guys. I'm the only girl on the court, and we have a great time (I'm on my school team and the guys all think I'm a great player). Here's my problem: I've got a major crush on one of the guys, but he just sees me as a friend. I think sometimes he forgets I'm even a girl! I love playing b-ball with these guys, but this crush is making me miserable. How can I get him to notice me, for _real_?

One of the Guys
New York

Dear One,
Before he stops seeing you as one of the guys,
you're going to have to show him that you're
also *one of the girls!* Maybe you should make
sure to be around him somewhere besides
the basketball court—somewhere you can
flirt your head off and make brilliant conversation. Do you have any classes together?
The same lunch period? How about inviting
all the guys to your place some day after a
game and talking about something besides
the NBA and Shaq's stats!

Joni

Dear One,
Borr-rring! If he sees a basketball every time he looks
at your face, nothing's going to change until you do
something *dramatic!* Get the lead in the school play.
Start a big campaign to clean up the environment.
Pierce your tongue and dye your hair purple. On
second thought, scratch that last one. It might turn
him off so much that he'd refuse to even play basketball with you. Anyway, you get the picture.

Su-Su

Dear One,
I agree with both my friends. Right now your relationship seems pretty one-dimensional. I also think you need to show him that you're a caring person. After all, that's what romance is all about, isn't it? Two people caring about each other. What do you care about? For instance, if it's all the stray pets at the animal shelter, call the shelter and see if they need volunteers to come in on weekends to walk the dogs. If they say yes, ask him if he'd like to volunteer, too. Even if he doesn't, you'll be doing something special, and he'll see you in a whole new light.
                                    Crystal
                        ♡

Dear Boy Talk,
My boyfriend and I were on the phone last night when he got another call. He put me on hold and when he came back he said, "Sorry, Veronica." And I said, "So who's Veronica?" My name doesn't sound anything like that. He tried to deny it, but I know what I heard. He has no sister named Veronica either. Do you think I should trust him?

                        Who's Veronica?

Dear Who's,
Definitely not! If it was all so innocent, he would have explained who Veronica was. I think he's up to something. Have you noticed anything else suspicious? Something that may have seemed like nothing at the time? Don't break up with him yet, though. Keep an eye on him. If he's really cheating, he'll slip up again.

Joni

Dear Who's,
Wow! If you take her advice, you could be losing an innocent guy forever. Has it occurred to you that it might have been a slip of the tongue? Male pride made him try to cover it up (that's so typical!), and you made such a big deal about it that he couldn't back down. Give your poor guy a second chance. Okay?

Crystal

Dear Who's,
I guess I'd have to go along with Crystal on this one. I mean, boyfriends are too hard to get for you to dump one over something so trivial. You might let him know that you're hurt, though. If he's really innocent, he'll do everything he can to prove how much he loves you—and that could be fun!

Su-Su

Dear Boy Talk,
Help! I met this guy who I thought was really cool at first. He asked me out to dinner and I said yes. I got all dressed up and he took me to a fast-food place. Then he didn't even pay for me. And afterward, when we went to a movie, he asked me to pay for both of us because he ran out of money! I don't mind paying for half, but this made me really steamed. He asked me out! If he asks me out again, should I go?

Not a Cheap Date
Texas

Texas

Dear Not Cheap,
You didn't say if you liked this guy. Was he fun to talk to? Did you have a good time? Maybe he had some big extra expenses after he asked you out and he was afraid to tell you because you might break the date. If the rest of the date was okay, I'd give him a second chance.

Crystal

Dear Not Cheap,
What a cheapskate! He's just lucky you brought some money along. If he invited you, then he should have known how much it would cost and been ready to pay. I think this guy is bad news. You'd be better off without him.

So-So

Dear Not Cheap,
If who pays is the only thing that would keep you from going out with him again, be up-front about it. Tell him how upset you were that he didn't tell you in advance he wasn't picking up the tab. If he says he can't afford to pay your half, then you can decide if going out with him is "worth it."

Joni

Dear Boy Talk,
Last night I went to a party with my boyfriend. While he was off with some of his friends, I kissed a guy who goes to another school. I'm scared my boyfriend will find out. But I like the other guy, too. Should I tell my boyfriend?

Makeout Queen
West Virginia

Dear Makeout,
What makes you think your boyfriend will find out that you kissed the other guy? Is he a detective or something? You said the new guy goes to another school. Maybe you should do some sleuthing on your own. You need to find out if he already has a girlfriend, because if he does, you could be wasting your time on him.

Joni

☎ Dear Boy Talk ‿‿‿‿‿‿‿‿‿‿‿

Dear Makeout,
Some people have all the luck! Two guys. Wow! My question is: Who's the best kisser? Your old boyfriend or the new guy? I definitely think you should find a way to do more research in this important area. You might want to change boyfriends. And even if you don't, two boyfriends are better than one!

Su-Su

Dear Makeout,
Shame on you! I don't think you should have sneaked around on your boyfriend and kissed somebody else. But on the other hand, I don't think you ought to rat on yourself either. That could be dangerous! Your boyfriend might be so mad and so hurt that he would break up with you. Then you wouldn't have anyone to kiss! Keep your lips sealed or your name could be *Leftout*!

Crystal